CHRISTMAS MARKET REUNION

KIM SMART

I dedicate this book to my friends and family for sharing your stories, to my past and future chance encounters, though not all on foreign soil, on sacred land indeed, and for all you gentle readers who have had, or long to have, your own chance encounters that leave you awestruck, breathless and grateful.

1

———

MIAMI ~ 2002

"Hal, can I freshen up your coffee?" Brooke asked politely. As a middle manager, Brooke Linton was not used to playing this role; but tonight, as the creative team assembled to save the company's bacon, she would do whatever she could to get her work noticed. She liked this company and would love to move up the ranks.

"Thanks Brooke. Say, how are your plans shaping up for your vacation? That's just right around the corner, isn't it? What a horrible time for us to be dragging you in here late every night to help *Menton Hotels*."

"Plans are coming along nicely. You know I'm taking my parents, right? We are all looking forward to the time together. Working on this account, and the new *Setting Tables* franchise, has given me the extra benefit of collecting enough miles to fly to London on the Concorde. I heard you and Dave talking about it last summer and it whetted my appetite."

"Rumor has it they are retiring their fleet next year. I'm glad you'll get the chance to fly with them before it's no longer possible. It's nice to be treated so well and you don't have to sit with all those strangers for hours on end. You will be amazed at how quickly you get into London."

I

"That's also what I heard when I made my reservations. I'm flying from here to New York at the end of next week. Then the Concorde will take me to London and I will drive to Germany to meet my parents."

"Let's see, your parents are in Kansas, right?"

"That's right. I'm surprised you knew that."

"It was one of many details that stood out to me in your resume. You went to Kansas University. I've followed their college football team some. I used to quarterback for my alma mater, Boston College."

"A powerful rival there."

Brooke turned to her supervisor, Bob Stone. "More coffee, Bob?"

"Thanks Brooke. Thanks for staying. I appreciate your support. *Menton* has been a long-time client, and the declining economy in their markets hit them hard in recent years. I don't know if this last ditch effort to rebrand them will help, but having the support of you and others on the team makes the effort more rewarding."

"You're welcome, Bob. I've loved working with their marketing team. In the last five years I have seen them step up their game. It's too bad the economy hasn't been as responsive."

"I think their multinational presence complicates the picture. It would be one thing if it were one part of their business suffering. The rest could carry the group for a while. Here, they had several losses because of the economy and those hurricanes. Isabel tore up the east coast, damaging several of their properties. Fabian devastated their luxury hotels in Bermuda. Insurance will help them some but it won't cover all their losses and lost profits entirely."

Bob picked up a set of sketches from the pile of papers on the conference table. The executive conference room had become a war room this week.

Martin-Hadley, a business development and consulting firm in Miami, was well respected and known for its tireless, personable approach to client matters. CEOs and owners often called them in for crisis management. *Menton Hotels* had forecast a financial downturn five years before and reached out to Martin-Hadley. Brooke was hired fresh out of college. Young and enthusiastic, with preceptorship experience at a similar firm in the Midwest, she was a great fit for the team dedicated to this account. Recently, she transitioned more time to a new account, *Setting Tables*, a restaurant chain featuring fresh, organic foods. It was a smaller account, but the firm gave Brooke the opportunity to elevate to a manager position on this design team.

"Just goes to show, a single event can cause you to change course at a moment's notice."

"That's right, and it can happen to anyone at any time." Bob studied the images. His brow furrowed as he dropped them back on the table. "We're missing something here. I'm just not feeling excited about the things I'm seeing. Too bad you will be gone. I believe you could help shape this campaign. You're full of fresh ideas, and this might just be the place for us to use them."

"I appreciate your vote of confidence, Bob." Brooke nodded toward the mock-ups lying on the table. "I see your concerns."

The sketches were sophomoric examples of the firm's usual superior work. They depicted uninviting marketing colors and layouts, proposed facade updates that displayed nothing attractive to entice guests to stay at the hotels, and offered a new stratification of properties. The sketches showed five levels of pricing and amenities.

"I've ordered Chinese takeout tonight. It should be here in twenty minutes or so. Pizza two nights in a row is not good for the soul," Hal announced. "Take a break, call your families and tell the little ones goodnight. Remember, there will be a bonus for all of you. We're tracking your hours and I appreciate you all."

Brooke admired Hal. It was delightful to work for a man of his caliber. He valued his team members and it showed. His integrity was unmatched. The firm commanded top rates but their output was worth every cent. Hal Martin and his wife, Marissa Hadley, founded the firm nearly thirty years ago and built an international following.

"Tell you what. I have some sketches from my early days with *Menton*. Let me look through those during dinner break. There might be some inspiration in my files."

"Magnificent idea Brooke. Thanks." Bob wrote some notes on his notepad. Brooke saw his stress. This account was important for the firm. The clients became friends, and he didn't want to let them down.

IN HER OFFICE, Brooke pulled several files up on her computer. Her colleague, Matt Brost, had apparently done the same thing to produce the mock-ups the crisis team reviewed. She had similar documents from him in her files from years prior.

Digging deep into the historical files, Brooke found more promising documents. Unlike Matt's proposed five-tiered accommodations, she had limited hers to three: high-end luxury in targeted international cities, family and business hotel accommodations to include some weekly rental suites with kitchens, and beachfront resorts with spas in known resort communities. Each tier had targeted images and colors in the marketing materials. Proposed property enhancements were limited to front entrance décor, with live plants specific to the property. Light, neutral interiors with spots of blue hues, signifying authority and stability, and purple for royalty and affluence, distinguished the luxury resorts reserved for crowds that expected such. These locations catered to the ultra-wealthy and dignitaries in places like Tel Aviv, Venice, Paris and New York.

Menton's largest collection of properties fell into the second group. These hotels catered to families and business travelers throughout the world. Designs were savvy, chic, and modern. Décor had a regional theme; with a minimalist feel created by the use of natural materials. The business line used green, orange, and yellow to bring professionalism together with friendly and happy vibes. Features included light woods and décor featuring green for calm and harmony, with spots of pink accents for romance and peace.

Brooke quickly edited the documents with suggestions based on what was already incorporated into these properties, several of which she had visited in recent years. This would lower implementation costs for *Menton*. She printed several color copies of the sketches and collated them into presentation folders for the group.

Team members regrouped in the conference room after making calls and eating dinner. It was nearly 8:00 p.m. and they planned to work another two hours. Brooke spotted Hal and Bob huddled in a corner. She approached them and handed each a presentation packet.

"I dusted off some old mock-ups and refreshed the images and cost projections. Just another idea for you to look at."

"Thanks Brooke." Bob and Hal eagerly opened their packets and studied the information.

"Okay folks. Let's gather up." Hal smiled and nodded to Brooke.

"Brooke has brought some additional concepts to the table for us to consider. Brooke, could you walk us through the material here?"

Brooke invited the team to open the presentation folders and walked them through the material. The group listened attentively to her concepts and studied the images.

"Thanks, Brooke," Hal announced when she was done. "I think there are some workable ideas in here. For the next hour, let's break into groups of three, find an office to work in and propose refinements to the ideas presented. We'll reconvene here at nine. Brooke, please join Bob and I in your office."

In her office, the small group made some slight refinements to the mock-ups and projections based on a similar project Hal and Bob had worked on before Brooke was hired. She approved of the enhancements and was thrilled they saw value in her work. "I know it's important that the designer be available for the presentation to *Menton*. If it's in the best interest of the company, I will cancel my vacation and find another time to go."

"There is no way I would allow you to do that, Brooke. If there is anything you have learned from me, it should be that your life needs balance. You are a hard worker. Don't think we haven't noticed! But you need this time away with your parents. I know you have a great trip planned with them and this is your chance to fly on the Concorde. You can't pass up that opportunity. Your materials here are nearly perfect now. There is time for Bob and I to get up to speed for a presentation. We'll probably bring Matt along to add some of his concepts, just to offer them some choice, but we will lean heavily on what you've prepared here."

"I echo Hal's comments, Brooke. You worked long hours, producing great product. Everyone needs time away to renew their creativity. Don't cancel a thing!"

The trio returned to the conference room and facilitated a round robin where each team shared their ideas. There was substantial support for Brooke's proposal with some minor enhancements. Matt was noticeably put off by the attention to Brooke and the praise for her work from the highest level of the organization. He sat in the shadows of the group with arms folded across his chest, staring at the table. He offered no input when his group presented their ideas.

Brooke stayed until midnight, alone in the office. When she became a manager, she graduated from a dreary interior cubicle to an outside office with floor to ceiling glass. She stood in front of the windows, looking down from the 32nd floor onto the Bay. Bright pink and yellow lights danced off the water below between streaming light reflections in purple and blue hues. The light show below was the exclamation point on the joy Brooke felt.

The pull to cancel her trip was not gone, but she knew how much her parents were looking forward to their first international trip. Her paternal great-grandfather was an immigrant, and her father longed to see the Bavarian countryside. To make the trip affordable, Brooke had scheduled it between Oktoberfest and the opening of Christmas Markets. Her dad would have preferred to go to Oktoberfest, and her mom to the Christmas Markets.

Brooke felt joy settled in. Being recognized for her talent by the top leaders in the company was a milestone. She now saw the way paved to becoming a Director in the company, a role with significantly higher status, pay, and perks. She was a shoo-in. The remaining question was, when would there be an opening?

2

———

"Thanks for meeting with me for lunch, Matt. I thought about how the pitch proposals went last week and I want to check in with you before I leave on vacation. I hope there are no hard feelings. I didn't mean to steal your thunder."

"Honestly Brooke, it felt a little slippery the way you swooped in and just happened to have some ideas to propose. We knew a month ago this crisis was brewing. If you had ideas, it seems they would have been brought forward before. It's like you were standing in wait to shoot down any ideas that were brought up."

"Whoa! I appreciate you being honest, but that's not how it came down. First, you know I'm not working with this client much since they promoted me to manager. Most of my time is spent on a new client. There would be no reason for me to be on notice of last week's crisis meetings. Second, the company always prefers the concept developers be the ones to pitch the ideas. I'm leaving at the end of the week for a pre-paid trip out of the country with my parents and won't be available to meet with the client."

"I can't believe you didn't cancel your trip. This is a Hail Mary for the client, and Martin-Hadley stands to gain a lot of goodwill and exposure in the industry if we can pull this off."

Brooke clenched her jaw. She was not inclined to share the

heart-to-heart message their bosses had showered on her. It was a pivotal moment in her relationship with them and one that she held on to as a representation of her value to them.

"I understand why you would say that, but that's just the way it is. I could see that Hal and Bob were not inspired by the ideas that were on the table. Like you, I had old ideas to dust off and bring to the table. I think your ideas were fine, if *Menton* was at a different stage in their journey. My ideas for consolidation and bolder branding are less costly and potentially more impactful."

"We will just have to accept a difference of opinion on our approaches."

"That's fine. I hope we can move past this. Our teams need to see our willingness to collaborate for the sake of the client." Brooke would leave it to Bob or Hal to tell Matt that he would help pitch the fresh ideas to *Menton*'s team. They would deal with the fallout if he could not conform to a collaborative stance.

"I agree. We are both professionals and will continue to model that for our staff."

"Besides, you're probably up next for a promotion, right? That would take you away from the *Menton* account and give you an extra project, don't you think? You've been a manager there for what, a year now?" Brooke did not see Matt as having promotion potential, but if he was looking, maybe she could get him to share ideas about where upcoming openings were.

"I heard that Jeff Cuddy, Director of Business Development might be leaving."

"No! I had no idea. He is highly respected here. He's been with the company for what, ten years?"

"Twelve. This is rumor, so keep it to yourself. He has cancer and has changed his lifestyle completely, hoping that reducing the stress will help him fight longer."

"Oh no! That's so sad to hear. I've always looked up to him for his contribution in meetings."

"I also heard that the new Director over design is not performing well."

"Shelly? She's looked a little stressed lately. I think she inherited an unhappy team when she joined the firm. It's too bad if she's not succeeding. Seems like it may not be all her fault."

"I agree, but I have heard that she's too inexperienced to handle the dysfunction in that group. She's trying, but she's too green to provide the right inspiration to turn the ship."

"It seems you would be a great fit for that role. Did you ever think of applying?"

"When it first opened, earlier in the year, I didn't apply. I was new enough in my current position that I felt like I needed more experience to be a viable candidate. Then, more recently, after hearing about Shelly's struggles, I had second thoughts. I was hoping I would be more well-received last night and could be taken seriously as a candidate. You seem to have made a name with the bosses so it may be less of a possibility for me."

"Matt, I'm sorry. I had no intention of upsetting your plans. I think you would be spectacular in that position. You have impressive management skills and you know the design world."

"Thanks for your vote of confidence. Unfortunately, it doesn't count to the hiring team."

"If they ask me, I will support you." Brooke rose and continued as she gathered her things. "Thanks again for meeting with me. I have to go meet with Bob now. My team will report to him when I'm gone, and he needs a heads-up on some recent developments. I hope you know, Matt, you've got my support."

BROOKE WAS RELIEVED to have this lunch meeting over with. With a full paper coffee cup and pleased with the new information gained, she headed up the elevator to her office. She gathered several documents and walked over to Bob's office.

"Come on in, Brooke. Have a seat." Bob pointed to the small conference table in the corner. "Thank you again for your input last week on the *Menton* project. I am grateful for your support even though you're not on that project any longer. We value your experience with them over the years."

"You're welcome, Bob. I'm glad I remembered those old files

and could bring them up to speed. How are things coming together for the presentation next week?"

"I'm pleased with where we are. There are some superstars on the design team that had excellent input on the presentation materials, so we will be ready."

"That's great to hear. I'm happy I could help, even if I can't be here for the big pitch. You and Hal will do a fantastic job, and with Shelly's team supporting you now, you'll knock it out of the park."

Brooke watched for Hal's reaction when she mentioned Shelly's name. He looked from Brooke to the conference table, then back to Brooke. She didn't want to read too much into it, but there was a reaction. Brooke talked Bob through her team's projects, upcoming vacations and the performance issue she was managing with one team member.

"That's what's going on. The team agrees to be on their best behavior. They have plenty of work to keep them busy. As we move into the holiday season, our client has several projects they want wrapped up and our plan reflects that. My assistant, Monica Ohms, manages that and can share that if you have a need."

"How is Monica doing? I know she had to take time off to help her mom through cancer treatment. Are things better now?"

"Her mother got through treatment okay and is doing well. She is not staying with Monica any longer. There are some financial struggles, but they don't seem to take Monica away from the office. She has children, and fortunately her husband works the night shift so they can cover for one another if a child gets ill and can't go to school. Monica tends to be moody, but she does brilliant work."

"I can't imagine the stress she's been under. I'll try to be gentle on her."

"Thanks Bob. If there's nothing else, I'll get back to my office. I have some assignments to take care of before I take off."

"Just one more thing. How have you left it with the clients? Do they know you're going on vacation?"

"They do. Monica has my cell number if she needs to reach me for anything urgent. My email and office phones will have out-of-office messages on them."

"Great. I hope Monica has no reason to contact you. Things should run smoothly. I know that's what you aim for as an influential leader. By helping our employees be their best, we also help them solve their own problems."

"My team is exceptional at that, yet they also come together well for collective creating. I love the entire team."

As BROOKE WALKED from Bob's office back to her own, she passed Jeff Cuddy's office and the desk of his assistant, Ginny. She rarely saw her or spoke to her, but today Brooke acted as if they were old friends. "Hey Ginny! How are you?"

"Oh, hey Brooke. Good. How are you?"

"Great. I was in visiting Bob before I take off on vacation at the end of the week. How about you? Any vacation coming up for you during the holiday season?"

"Well, you probably know that things are up in the air here with Jeff being out on extended leave. Honestly, I don't know from one day to the next what's going on. Sylvia has stepped in as acting Director for now."

"Is there some concern he won't be back?"

Ginny leaned in and lowered her voice. "It's not news for public consumption yet, but Hal will announce Jeff's resignation next week. Jeff has decided to really try to kick cancer's butt, so he will stop working and focus solely on taking care of himself. He's got some nutrition guru and big name cancer specialists working with him."

"Oh, my goodness, Ginny! I had no idea it was that serious. Do you think Sylvia will step into the Director role full time then?"

"No way! She doesn't want to be the boss. She loves what she does and isn't looking for more stress."

"I get it. It's good to know your limits."

"Honestly, I'm not sure what they will do with the position after Jeff leaves. Personnel asked me to review the job description, and I gave them some feedback. I assume they will post the position."

"Well, I'm glad they have you here with all your experience on the team. That will help with whatever transition comes down the pike."

"Thank you. I hope you enjoy your vacation, Brooke. Where are you going?"

"I'm taking my parents to Germany. It's a lifelong dream for them. I love to travel. Do you like chocolate? I hear they have excellent chocolate products where we're going."

"I do. What a treat that would be! You and your folks have a wonderful time." Ginny waved Brooke off as she turned to answer the phone.

BACK IN HER OFFICE, Brooke checked for messages. A message from her youngest sister Lana, with the subject line BIG ANNOUNCEMENT, caught her attention. Reading on, she found an invitation to a family conference call for a special announcement. The call was scheduled for Thursday evening, two days before Brooke's departure.

Brooke ran through the list of potential news items from princess Lana, the favored child and youngest of four girls. Good luck always rained down on Lana. She was born a beautiful child, and the more she aged the more stunning she became. Now, at twenty-four, she had an Ivy League education that she raced through because school was easy for her; she landed a high-paying executive position with a marketing firm right out of college through her sorority connections; and her part-time modeling career afforded her a luxury apartment in the heart of Atlanta. She wasn't dating anyone. Their mother would have shared that with Brooke. Maybe she got a new job and was moving, Brooke speculated.

Before she got home from work that evening, she already had a message from her mother inquiring about what Brooke thought the big news could be. Lana wasn't taking their mother's calls. She was undoubtedly holding out for a dramatic announcement.

3

———

On Thursday evening, Brooke was still in the office when the time came for the family conference call. Lana arranged for a NetMeeting call using their respective computers. Julie and Robin, the two oldest sisters, and Brooke peered in on Lana, who sat on a sheepskin rug on a pink velveteen sofa in her living room. The video image jumped around if there was too much movement, and the audio was delayed at times, but it was a decent way to communicate with the group.

"Thank you all for joining me. I'm sorry we couldn't all be together for this special announcement, but I'm glad you're here. Mom, Dad, I can't see you. Did you follow the instructions I sent to plug in your new computer camera for this video call?"

"Just a minute, dear. Your father is on the floor looking at the back of the tower thingy." Suddenly the group got a close-up view of their mother, leaning into the camera.

"Mom, sit back in your chair, I can see down your blouse." Robin was the most direct of all the girls. The oldest at thirty-four, she lived the farthest away. She moved to the suburbs of New York City shortly after high school. Known as the creative in the family, she produced indie films. She started as an apprentice, working at a coffee shop to pay her share of the rent in an over-crowded one-bedroom apartment and writing articles for magazines. Today, she was well respected in her field, but would never produce a blockbuster movie, nor did she want to. Robin was the direct opposite of Lana, who craved the limelight. Robin preferred to lurk in the shadows, forming judgments and opinions on everyone and everything she met, sharing them freely without warning.

"Okay Mom, we see you. Can you see me?" Lana smiled and waved.

"There you are, dear. Oh my, I can see you all if I just click here on this box." Their mother, Linda, was somewhat familiar with computer operations from her part-time work as the church secretary. Frank, their father, was a total Luddite. He preferred to be in the middle of the dairy herd or on his tractor rather than sitting behind a computer.

"There you are, my beautiful girls!" Frank was the most reserved in the bunch. Brooke often wondered if he was born that way or if it was a byproduct of being the only man with five women in one house. Frank loved his children equally. He never showed favoritism, unlike Linda who favored the youngest child the most.

"Hi Dad! It's good to see you. Thanks for getting the camera set up. Now, I don't want to keep you waiting. I know everyone is busy. I bet you've been guessing why I called you all together and Mom, I know you've reached out to everyone to see what's going on, but nobody knows but me... and..."

Lana paused and reached to her left, pulling in a man who had been sitting just outside the camera's view. "Everyone, I want you meet Dr. Pablo Porta."

There was a mixed response from the group, all at the same time.

"Hello Dr. Porta, nice to meet you."

"Hi, Pablo."

"Hey there."

Pablo's light brown skin, wide-set almond eyes, dark wavy hair and broad, cleft chin were a complimentary contrast to Lana's petite, heart-shaped face, fair complexion and long blonde curls.

"Hello everyone. It's nice to meet you all."

"Hi, I'm Julie." Julie worked as a librarian in Kansas City. She was thirty-two, married with two children, a dog and a white picket fence. She was the most like their parents. Although she lived close, she spent little time with Linda and Frank. Her in-laws were dominant in her life and demanded her attention.

"Brooke here. Nice to meet you." Brooke waved to the camera and smiled.

"Robin. Hi."

"And we are the parents, Linda and Frank. Nice to meet you Dr., uh, Pablo." Linda looked at Frank for his input, and then smiled at the camera.

"There now, you've all met. Pablo and I have some big news." Lana turned to Pablo and together they made the announcement. "We're getting married!"

The couple's dazzling smiles lit up the screen.

Linda drew in her breath and clasped her hands. "Oh, honey, congratulations!"

She looked at Frank, her eyes begging him to show enthusiasm for the news.

"Congratulations Lana, Pablo. This is very exciting news!" Frank was happy for Lana, but had secretly dreaded this day, from a financial perspective. Lana was his champagne daughter. She was the one daughter who had insisted on trendy clothes and the latest hairstyles when she was growing up on their dairy farm.

The sisters all chimed in with their congratulatory messages. This would be the second marriage amongst the four of them. Julie's wedding was a low budget affair with hand-made bridal party dresses and a church basement reception with finger sandwiches, punch and an overly sweet layer cake. Lana's would certainly be a more extravagant affair.

"Have you started making any plans? Do you know when and where you will marry?" Linda was the planner for the family and didn't want to miss an opportunity to get in on the early planning.

Lana's petite hands moved up to encircle Pablo's biceps. "The Waldorf here had a cancellation for December 31st. Pablo and I both have time off for the New Year so we snatched up that opening. I know it's soon, but we have a fantastic wedding planner who assured us she's had shorter planning times and can pull this together."

Frank felt the blood drain from his face as he wondered what a wedding planner would cost on top of the Waldorf.

"We hope you can all accommodate the short notice and join us. We are inviting only family and our closest friends. We're planning for 200 guests." Pablo seemed invested in the wedding plans. He put his hand over Lana's. "We will take our honeymoon in Turks and Caicos for a week."

"Well, it sounds like you have everything planned, and so quickly." Linda tried not to show her disappointment. Her daughter's wedding was a highly emotional investment for her.

"Mom, I know how much you love to plan a party, but since we are so far apart and the time is so short, I felt I just needed to jump in and get it done." Lana anticipated her mother's disappointment and her father's concern for the price tag. "Dad, the good news for you is that Pablo and I are paying for everything. We don't expect you to do anything but show up and have a fabulous time. We even have rooms blocked at the hotel for our families the night of the wedding."

"Ah, well, that's nice of you, but you know we want to do our part." Frank didn't want to seem too relieved, but he was very relieved.

"We appreciate that, Mr. Linton…"

"Please, call me Frank."

"We appreciate that, Frank, but we are both at a place in our careers where we can easily manage the expenses. Save your money for traveling. I hear you are taking a big trip soon and then we will want to see you for the wedding."

"That's very generous of you." Linda knew they had to raid

their wedding fund for the girls time and again through the years to keep the ranch afloat. There was about $20,000 available and three daughters yet to marry.

"Robin, I hope your production schedule will allow you to join us. We have a highly recommended videographer lined up to film the ceremony."

"We have a production scheduled then, but I'm sure I can take time off to come. Thank you for the invitation." Robin did not enjoy fancy events. If she couldn't wear her well-worn cargo pants, she was not interested in attending, but for her sister, and her parents, she would be there.

"Thank you. It means a lot to us for all of you to be here. Julie, I presume you will be on a Christmas break schedule. Is that right?"

"Yes, we will be. Keith and I were planning to take the girls skiing, but we can work around that and make a vacation out of our road trip to Atlanta."

"Wonderful! We look forward to seeing the entire family. If it's okay with the girls, we will have special responsibilities for them."

"Of course. They would love to have special jobs. Send me details on what they need for clothes and stuff and we will be ready."

"Will do." The nieces, seven and nine, would fit right into Lana's plan for an elegant princess-type affair. Both girls were fair and pretty. She envisioned them in tulle and sparkles.

"Brooke, that just leaves you. We know you are married to your job and understand if you cannot join us, but please know that we would love for you to join us."

Brooke nearly rolled her eyes, but remembered that she had an audience. She saw her mother bite her lower lip, probably praying Brooke wouldn't react to Lana's comments. Could Lana be more condescending? "I will be there. I wouldn't miss it for the world! Mom, Dad, and I will return from our trip overseas weeks before, and the firm generally takes a break with the turn of the year. We will have completed the year-end work for our clients and finished the New Year planning."

"Wonderful! The entire family will be here!" Lana beamed with excitement.

"Pablo, will your family be there? Can you tell us anything about them?" Linda was a bit put off that she hadn't met his parents. She didn't even know there was a Pablo in her daughter's life! She looked forward to a follow-up call with just Lana to get more details.

"My adoptive mother lives in Chicago. She will be here for the wedding. My sister, Annabelle, is deployed to Afghanistan. I'm afraid she won't be able to join us."

"And your father?" Linda was a traditionalist. Every family had a mother, father, two children and a dog.

"My mother raised us as a single mom. She was so busy dedicating herself to Annabelle and I that she never took the time to find herself a partner. I'm grateful to have found my partner in Lana. You all know how wonderful she is and I need you to know how deeply I love her."

"Can you tell us anything about how you met and your engagement story?" Julie was the romantic. She loved a fairytale with a happy ending.

"It's a sweet story, really. We met on a blind date set up by a mutual friend. Actually, a former boyfriend of Lana's introduced us. He was a colleague of mine at a local hospital who took a job in California. He was always talking about this wonderful woman he dated before he moved away. He set us up on a blind date."

"Troy is a good guy but he knew I didn't want to leave Atlanta and my job. We are still good friends. He will be coming to the wedding. We can't thank him enough for making the introduction."

"That sounds very sweet. I, for one, am just a little surprised we never heard of Pablo before. I mean, I at least heard of Troy from Mom." Robin wasn't beating around the bush. This was a fast courtship, and she wanted to know why.

"It has been a bit of a whirlwind here. Pablo and I knew, from the moment we met, that we were destined to be together. He proposed on our third date, and everything has fallen into place quickly. Neither of us needs a long courtship. We just feel so right together." Pablo reached over, planted a kiss on Lana's cheek and smiled at the video camera.

Robin typed out a text message to Brooke. *Think she's prego?*

Brooke smiled and replied. She wondered too. *No way. She would have flown the blimp past those enormous picture windows to tell us if that was the case.*

Robin responded. *You're right. He feels like a player to me.*

Brooke couldn't agree more, but she would not bring drama to the table, for their mother's sake. She would silently observe and be there to help Linda when Lana's world fell apart.

"We are so happy to meet you, Pablo. We will properly welcome you to the family when we see you in person. Lana, honey, we will talk more. I want to hear all about your dress, and everything."

"I would ask you to come out for a weekend and shop with me Mom, but I know you're traveling with Brooke. I'll send you pictures of the things I like. I know how much you like this sort of thing." Lana already had her dress chosen, invitations ordered, bridesmaids and their dresses selected and the reception planned. There was nothing left for her mother to do, but she would send her pictures anyway, to keep in her favor.

"That's sweet, honey. I guess the timing just wasn't right for me to come there to help you."

Robin sent another text to Brooke. *She plays Mom like a fiddle. Mom wouldn't even get a vote, even if she could go shopping. I hope you have a wonderful time on your trip and all this hoopla doesn't distract them from having fun.*

Thanks. I'm sure we will have fun. Dad, especially, has been looking forward to this for a long time.

They all said their goodbyes and the video call was over. Brooke gathered her things and left the office.

. . .

By the time she got home, the funk was setting in. Another sister getting married and Brooke hadn't had a date in months. When could she? She was working all the time. Yet, she silently hoped someone would find her magnetically attractive and pursuable.

In her mind, Brooke reviewed the videoconference with Lana. Her eyes swelled as she recalled the excitement in her mother's voice, the syrupy tone she used to compel Pablo to share his family story. Her mother didn't show that much excitement about any aspect of the upcoming trip. It felt to Brooke that no matter what she did, she would always be one-upped by someone or something - usually lovely Lana.

4

---

*B*rooke's head filled with ideas as she lay down to sleep. She finally drifted off about 3 a.m. and woke at 6 with a resurgence of energy. She had one day left in the office before vacation and she needed to make it count. This was a critical time for the organization, and for Brooke professionally. With potential vacancies coming open, she devised a strategy to keep her name relevant with the hiring team. She would need her assistant to help her out.

"Good morning, Monica. I hope you had a great evening." Brooke presented Monica with her favorite coffee drink.

"Good morning, Brooke. The kids and I had a fantastic time. It seems like from now through the end of the year they have plays and concerts, sporting events and awards activities. Somewhere in there I'm supposed to do shopping and holiday decorating."

"Maybe I can help. How about if I pick up some souvenirs from my trip and you can add them to their Christmas stockings? What kinds of things do they like?"

"That would be nice, Brooke, but unnecessary. Forget them! I would love to have a Christmas ornament from Germany. A wooden one."

"You've got it! I'll look around for something the kids might like, too."

"Thanks. Now, what's on your list of things to finish up before you leave? You're all caught up as far as I know and there are no meetings scheduled for today. Maybe you can get out of here and start your vacation early."

"That would be nice, but there is something I need to work on. Can you meet me in my office at eleven?"

"Sure thing, and thanks for the coffee."

"You're welcome. See you about eleven?"

"Yes. I'll be there. Need me to bring anything?"

"No. I think I've got what I need for now."

In her office, Brooke gathered evidence that she was the right person to take Jeff Cuddy's job when he retired. She emailed off to his assistant, Ginny, to see if she could get an underground copy of the job description for his replacement. Brooke felt strongly that she was prepared to take on an expanded role in the organization. She was ready to take on greater responsibility with the firm's overall direction, or so she thought. At only twenty-six, her experience was limited.

Ginny soon shot back an email. *Sorry for the delay, Brooke. I have attached my edited draft of Jeff's position description.* As she read through the responsibilities of the position, Brooke felt more and more assured she could handle the tasks outlined. She drafted a cover letter to address each element and provided an example of the many ways in which she believed she met the criteria.

As she sat thinking through her arguments to support a promotion, she devised statements against hiring co-workers who might apply for the position. She was deep in thought when Hal stopped by to wish her well on her trip. She thanked him and told him she hoped they could meet to discuss potential promotion opportunities when she returned. She wanted to launch into a diatribe about how she was the preferred candidate over all others, ready to enumerate their failures and highlight her successes, but thought better of that approach considering there was no current job opening.

By the time Monica arrived for their scheduled meeting, Brooke's cover letter was nearly finished.

"Hey, thanks for joining me, Monica. I can't believe the time has finally arrived for this big trip." Brooke looked up from her computer and turned to Monica sitting on the other side of the desk.

"It seems like just yesterday you started planning it. Time really flies." Monica was sick of hearing about this trip, but happy for Brooke to get a vacation. Brooke worked too hard, which in turn, made Monica's job hard. She regularly met with her own boss to discuss the heavy workload Brooke gave her, but because Brooke brought in money for the firm, nothing was ever done about it.

"Do you still have my credit card information?" Brooke leaned on Monica to manage not only her business travel and expenses, but some of her personal things as well.

"I do." Monica knew that question meant more work for her. She sighed silently while maintaining a smile in Brooke's direction.

"I have this list of activities to add to our itinerary. I've listed the events and the dates. My mom mentioned this opera she wants to see, I found a local farm-family hosted dinner event, and they both need some pampering. I know I've asked a lot of you for my trip, but I promise you, it will be worth your time." Brooke intended to buy something special for Monica while away, something more than souvenir chocolates or beer steins.

"Sure, just leave the list with me and I'll get to work on it this afternoon." It was not her nature to resist or set limits.

"There's one other thing. I know this is not public knowledge so please don't say anything, but Jeff Cuddy is going out on medical retirement."

"Oh, no! I knew about his cancer, but really hoped he would just need a little time off for treatment and come back."

"I'm sure he has his reasons and I wish him all the best, but it means there will probably be a vacancy coming up in the organization. They may post it while I'm away. I'm putting together a packet with a cover letter and my resume. If you see the posting, could you send it to my text messages? Then, if I see a need for edits in my letter, could I ask you to make those for me?"

"Wow, that's a big position, Brooke. I mean, Jeff's been with the company a long time. He started in the print and media shop way back when and worked his way up." Monica bit her lip. She didn't mean to sound negative, but she wasn't prepared for Brooke to take such a high level position. Monica wasn't sure what it meant for her.

"I would, of course, want you to stay with me as my assistant, if that's what you want." Brooke sensed Monica's hesitation, but assumed it was about her own status with the organization and not Brooke's relative inexperience in the industry.

"Yes. I would want to stay on with you. I'll keep my ears open for any news on the position opening up and let you know right away. I'm happy to make edits at your direction."

"Thank you, Monica. I knew I could count on you. We're in this together." Brooke walked around the desk. "I'll make my rounds with the team and then pack up to leave."

Monica stood beside Brooke, who put her arm around Monica's shoulders and escorted her to the door. "I really appreciate all you do to help me. Let me know if you have any problems with adding those extra events to our trip, will you?"

"I'll do my best."

Brooke smiled. "No doubt. You always do."

She walked down the hallway to check in with the rest of her team before she left the office. If things went well, Brooke could be looking at a new position when she returned from her trip.

Before leaving the office, Brooke called Lana. "Hey Lana. I just wanted to tell you congratulations again and let you know I appreciated the opportunity to meet Pablo last evening."

"Oh Brooke, thank you for calling! I hope the family loves him as much as I do. I truly am the luckiest girl alive. He thought you were all great." Brooke didn't know how Pablo could have formed that opinion in their brief interaction.

"I'm just so surprised we never heard you talk about Pablo before. I mean this all seems so sudden."

Lana laughed. "It is fast. Pablo says he's afraid I'll get cold feet if he doesn't get me to the altar as soon as he can."

"Well… that's sweet." Brooke mumbled, "I guess" under her breath. She didn't want to rain on Lana's parade, but she still felt something was off about the sudden proposal and acceptance. Lana would typically want to be showered with special events centered on her. It would be more like her to expect multiple elegant bridal showers and swanky bachelorette parties.

"The day will be here before I know it, and there's so much to do. I'm so grateful to have found a superb wedding planner who had an unexpected last-minute opening and agreed to take me as a client. It is all falling into place. I'm glad the actual date isn't when you planned to be out of the country. It would have been a shame for you to have to cancel your trip."

"Right. We are all thankful, too." It's just like Lana to believe they would have canceled their trip to accommodate her sudden plans. Actually, she probably would have won that battle. Brooke's family-driven guilt and their mother's commitment to her children would have won. "I know you have lots to do so I'll let you go."

"Okay. We have a cake tasting coming up and I need to get my preliminary selections to the baker. He's not my first choice but comes highly recommended by the Archibalds. You know, my boss? His wife is an avid party-thrower and knows all the best vendors. Pablo and I hope you all have a terrific vacation. We are cooking up a little something special for the folks while you are away. They will be thrilled when they get back to the farm."

Brooke decided not to bite on that teaser. She couldn't care less about Brooke and Pablo's surprise. She had her own special things planned for their parents. She hated to add more to her credit cards right now, but when she gets her promotion it will be a piece of cake to pay them off. Besides, she wanted the trip to be memorable for them all - something more than just a day of celebration, like Lana's wedding will be.

Brooke packed her briefcase, said her farewells and left the office. At home, she looked through the assortment of bon voyage gifts the team had given her during an impromptu office party a few days prior. She had plastic toiletries bottles, anti-diarrheal medicines, a first aid kit, a sewing kit, an extra flash drive for her camera, a disposable rain jacket, an international travel adapter, and two guidebooks. Most of these were duplicates. Brooke was a planner and had been making purchases for this trip for over six months. Looking through the pile one last time, she grabbed the amenities kits and rain jacket and tucked them into her suitcase.

WHILE WAITING for the car service to pick her up, Brooke called Robin to report on her conversation with Lana. "I'm telling you, I think there's something off about this rush to the altar. It's just not Lana's style."

"You're right, and frankly, I don't care. I'm not sure why you do. It's her life. Lana is Lana. She will do whatever she wants whenever she wants. Why would you expect that to change just because she's older? You, dear Brooke, need to leave all this drama and your work behind and have an outstanding time. Lord knows you've worked long and hard enough to enjoy time away. Think of all those weekends you spent with clients. I don't care that you were entertaining them at baseball games and art shows. That was still time that you can't get back. That's time that you donated to the company. Leave it behind, let your hair down and have some fun!"

"Spoken like the big sister you are. I'll do my best. Did I tell you I may have a shot at a promotion at the firm?"

"Hey, that's great! But remember, even if you aren't the chosen one, I love you and think you're awesome!" Robin knew the pressures Brooke put upon herself to be all to everyone. She anticipated their parents' needs and met them. She worked far more than her salary paid her for and rarely did anything for herself.

Robin recognized the pattern. She was that way once too, but learned that her happiness required that she break away and find herself, for herself. It took her far from home and down a creative path she would never have followed if she lived under the control of their conservative, work-driven parents. She wanted the same freedoms for Brooke, but knew she needed to find them on her own. The most Robin could do was to be there to support and encourage Brooke.

"You know we'll have a grand time. I hope to get some great photos and have a book made up before we meet up at the wedding. I'll give you a buzz when we get home and give you a blow-by-blow of our activities. You got the itinerary with phone numbers I emailed, right?"

"I sure did and I don't plan to make a single call to you while you're away so don't worry if you don't hear from me."

"I won't. Love you, sis. Thanks for being there."

"Love you, too. Have a blast!"

Brooke double-checked her carry-on bag and packed an extra wool shawl, just in case her mother forgot hers. One last check of the apartment ensured that windows were locked, shades drawn and lights off. She inhaled deeply and exhaled the residual tension from the office and her call to Lana. With a forced smile, she grabbed her bags and locked the door of the peaceful retreat she called home.

5

AMSTERDAM ~ 2002

The Concorde flight from New York to London was just over three hours long. Arriving in London at 8:00 a.m., Brooke enjoyed the luxury of the flight and lamented the relatively brief trip. From London she took a flight to Amsterdam. This was a splurge, the only solo vacation day on her itinerary. In Amsterdam, she would rent a car and drive to Frankfurt where she would meet her parents the following day.

Her seatmates on the flight to Amsterdam were a young couple traveling around the world. They put their careers on pause to explore people and places and perform volunteer work. They had worked on organic farms, on clean water development projects, at food distribution centers and at schools. They were now flying back home for an extended holiday break before resuming their travels.

"Our families live in the same small town outside Amsterdam. They will let us move in whenever we are ready to settle down. We will then find jobs and save for our own place and start our family. That's the tradition in our families."

Brooke responded with lukewarm interest. She silently criticized them for wasting their lives. She assumed there was something wrong with the relationships with their parents, seeing that they wouldn't settle down and get to work already.

"Please fasten your seatbelts and put your belongings away. We are preparing for our descent into Amsterdam Airport Schiphol. We will be landing in twenty minutes." Brooke was grateful for the flight attendant who interrupted the talk of her new acquaintances with their unfamiliar lifestyle. She just wanted to relax and be fully present in her adventure.

She turned to her seatmates. "It was nice to meet you. I wish you all the best on your adventure."

She hoped that was final enough for them to get the hint that she was done listening. It worked.

BROOKE STOOD at the luggage carousel until every piece of luggage was claimed. Hers was not there. The attendant at the airline counter took down the hotel information and promised to have the lost luggage delivered as soon as it arrived, which could be as late as the following day.

She wasn't going to let this minor mishap fluster her. She had identification, money, and credit cards, and that's all she needed to rent the car and start sightseeing. The time zones were messing with her energy a little. At home it was the middle of the night. She was tired but rode the wave of excitement as she started to explore the city.

BROOKED ASKED the rental car company for a map to the hotel. It was too early to check in, so she asked for recommendations for top areas for tourists.

"This area here..." the attendant pointed to an area inside a large red ink circle "...is the most popular place to visit. Anne Frank's house is here." He placed an X on the location.

"Thank you." Brooke gathered up the map and her carry-on. She found her assigned car in the lot and drove through the checkout exit. The hotel was near the tourist sites, so she drove to the hotel parking lot, left the car and walked around the area.

Brooke stopped in the middle of the sidewalk near a busy inter-
section. It was Saturday, and the markets were bustling with locals
stocking up on groceries. In navy and rust business casual clothes,
she stood out in the crowd of casually dressed locals. Brooke held
the map out, rotating it to match the street names.

A man approached her and spoke in perfect American English.
"May I help you find something?"

Brooke turned to see a handsome man, about thirty, casually
dressed in jeans, a knit sweater and sneakers. "Hi. Uh… I was
looking for Helen Keller's house."

Flustered and somewhat fatigued, she watched as a grin
spread across his face and his eyes sparkled.

"Um, I think you're in the wrong country for that. Do you
mean Anne Frank?" He could have burst out in a belly laugh but
didn't want to offend this beautiful, smartly dressed young
tourist.

Brooke laughed at her mistake, something that rarely came
easily to her. "Oh, my! Yes, I'm looking for Anne Frank's house."

She held her hand out. "I'm Brooke."

He took her hand in his. "Pleasure to meet you, ma'am. I'm
Bridger, Bridger Goins. I'm just headed that way myself. Mind if I
walk with you?"

Brooke looked up at the dark-haired man, nearly a head taller
than she with a lean, fit body. It seemed so odd that she would
meet an American first thing on her vacation. She laughed. "That
would be great. Then maybe you could explain to me how it is an
American man came to my rescue on the first day of my European
vacation."

"I'm not sure I can explain the synchronicity. All I can say is
that I'm glad we met and that I'm a tourist here today as well. I'm
in the Army, stationed outside of Munich. I've just come for a
brief sightseeing vacation." Bridger pointed to his left. "Here, I
think we should head in this direction."

Brooke put her map away and followed his lead. In a short

time they arrived at their destination. The two toured the Anne Frank house together. They marveled at the photos, videos and writings found at the home, the oppression of the times and the experience, and the perseverance required to keep the faith during such a difficult time. In anticipation of their tour, they had each read up on Anne Frank's writings and experience. It thrilled Brooke to have someone interesting, and handsome, to share the experience with. As they strolled along the Prinsengracht canal, they exchanged thoughts.

"Thank you for letting me tag along, Brooke." Bridger was grateful to have such a beautiful escort on his tour. He enjoyed the conversation. "I'm getting a little hungry. Would you care to join me for some lunch?"

"I would be delighted to have lunch. I am feeling a bit hungry myself and I will never pass up an opportunity to try something new." Brooke had noticed pastries in a shop window earlier and a sampling of their sweetness was on her mind.

They wandered into a small cafe nearby. There was a slight chill in the outside air so it felt good to be inside warming up. They ordered coffee with milk, a bowl of soup with a bread pretzel and dessert. Brooke's dessert was a chocolate-filled pastry and Bridger's was custard. They sampled each other's desserts.

"Now that's the richest creamy custard I have ever tasted! That's better than my mom's flan." Brooke knew she had just taken in an extra five hundred calories in the one small spoonful of the silky, dense custard. "I think I need to walk a couple miles to work these calories off, but it's worth every bite."

"I have a few other sites on my wish list. Would you like to come along? I think they're all walkable from here." Bridger pulled a small notebook from his shirt pocket while Brooke reached into her carry-on and pulled out her dog-eared guide-book. They compared notes and sketched out a plan for the afternoon.

Brooke felt safe and at ease with Bridger. "Is it odd that we just met and we're spending the day together?"

"Maybe, but you won't hear me complaining. I'm enjoying the company."

Bridger tucked his notebook back in his pocket. He paid the lunch bill and ushered Brooke back onto the street.

As they walked around De Wallen, the red-light district, Brooke learned that Bridger grew up in the Chicago area. He entered the army after college and liked his army career. He enjoyed traveling, and he liked his work. Brooke shared about her family and work.

The stroll in the De Wallen neighborhood took them down side streets along several canals. For Brooke and Bridger, the walk by the one hundred or so apartments satisfied their curiosity. The historic buildings in the area, including the Gothic-style Oude Kerk, the city's oldest church, were more interesting than what went on behind the windows with red lights burning in them.

Bridger wanted to visit the torture museum. Brooke wanted to see the floating flower market and stroll through the marketplace looking for small gifts to take home. She knew that it was early to be buying anything, but this was the only day she would be in Amsterdam. She found hand painted flower bulbs, wooden clog-shaped Christmas tree ornaments, chocolate, and licorice.

The two met up late in the afternoon where they originally met. They were about a half-mile from Brooke's hotel. "I would be happy to give you a lift to the hotel, if you don't mind riding in my beat up BMW. I picked up the old thing just for touring about. It's been reliable, but it's not very pretty."

"That would be great. I must admit that my feet could use the break. I usually wear my walking shoes for a city tour, but my luggage didn't arrive with me. Maybe it will be there now and I can check in."

They walked two blocks to Bridger's car. "I see what you mean. Looks like your car has seen some better days. If I didn't trust your judgment, I would worry about your safety in this thing."

Brooke couldn't remember when she had ridden in a beater like Bridger's.

"Well, at least you know I'm not too proud to share my junk with you. It's reliable. I have a buddy in the motor pool who looks after it for me. He assures me it's in good working order."

SURPRISINGLY, the car didn't have a single backfire, squeak or groan as they drove to the hotel. When they parked, Bridger barely had the key turned off before he jumped out to open the door for Brooke. Brooke had gathered her overnight bag and was just reaching for the door handle when Bridger opened the door. "Oh, thank you!" Brooke nodded at the hotel. She hadn't noticed its opulence when she first arrived. "Want to come see what's inside this beautiful building?"

She had splurged when she reserved the room for this one night in Amsterdam, where she wasn't also renting a room for her parents. The building was palatial with grand architecture that complemented the heritage buildings and parks around, and had an elegant lobby with multiple bars and restaurants.

"Good afternoon." A pleasant young woman with a broad smile greeted Brooke. Her hair was neatly swept into a stylish bun and her suit was crisply pressed. "May I help you?"

Brooke smiled back and introduced herself.

"Miss Linton, we are happy to have you here with us. Your luggage arrived a short time ago, and we placed it in your room for you. We are sorry you experienced the delay with your luggage and to show our concern for you, I have this gift coupon for a courtesy discount on dinner and drinks for two at the price of one in our dining room this evening."

Brooke was floored. She encouraged her clients to be generous with courtesy gifts, but this was above and beyond. The hotel was not responsible for her delayed luggage. "That's very kind of you. Thank you!"

Brooke took the room key, the coupon and turned to Bridger. "It seems I have received dinner for two on the hotel this evening. If it's not an inconvenience, maybe you would care to join me?"

"Are you kidding me? I would love to! My hotel is more ordinary than this. I wouldn't pass up the chance to have dinner with a beautiful woman in the lap of luxury. I'm sure you want to freshen up. How about if I go over to the bar there and wait for you?" Bridger pointed to a lounge area built around a fireplace.

"That sounds great. I'm getting hungry and I read that the food here is fantastic. I'll be about a half-hour."

6

$\mathcal{B}$rooke quickly showered, willing away the jet-lag tiredness, and changed into the one black dress she packed. She grabbed an emerald green wrap and black shoes. Thick, wavy, strawberry-blonde hair graced her shoulders. She dabbed light pink lipstick on and left the luxury of her room.

When Brooke got to the lobby, she didn't immediately see Bridger. He stood and waved from the nearby lounge. "You look refreshed and beautiful, Brooke."

Bridger had borrowed a dinner jacket from the hotel and looked dapper. They ordered cocktails, and munched on nuts and crackers brought to their intimate corner of the room. They recapped their day and the way things just fell into place.

"If I had wanted to plan a special day, I could not have topped this one." Bridger had a romantic streak. He hadn't mentioned his love life, other than to say he was a bachelor and wasn't seeing anyone. Brooke couldn't help but wonder why he was single. He seemed like quite a catch.

"You talked about your work and your family, but you never really mentioned anything about your social life other than church activities." Bridger was equally curious about Brooke, and bold enough to ask.

"That's because there's nothing to say. I don't really date

much. I'm pretty much married to my job." Brooke knew she was equally tethered to her family, but didn't want to admit that.

"I find it hard to believe that men are not knocking your door down. You're beautiful, obviously very smart and talented, nice, interesting, and did I mention beautiful?"

Brooke waved his words away. "Oh, stop! You'll make me blush."

"Seriously, if I was back in the States you wouldn't be able to get rid of me." They laughed at the thought of it. He wasn't in the States so it was an easy claim for him to make.

They chatted with the bartender, who spoke English well, and learned that the hotel was a hot spot for celebrities and big events. Brooke shared her planned itinerary and got some travel tips for her and her parents.

"If you go to the bar on the top floor after eight, they have karaoke. A lot of locals come in for that on the weekends. Check it out."

Brooke smiled and raised her eyebrows, inviting Bridger.

"I'm no singer. Even the church choir threw me out." He wasn't kidding. The choir director had nicely asked him to be in charge of the songbooks and chairs. He could not carry a tune, no matter how hard he tried. "I'll go, but I will NOT sing. I could not insult your senses that way."

Brooke smiled. "We'll see how we feel after dinner. I may be too tired myself." She loved karaoke in college, and had won some friendly competitions. Unlike Bridger, she didn't get kicked out of the church choir. She was occasionally the featured soloist.

They finished their cocktails as the lounge was filling up with hotel guests, and headed into the dining room for dinner. Brooke and Bridger appeared so comfortable together that the maitre d' mistakenly referred to them as a married couple. "Welcome to the Orb, mevrouw en meneer. Do we have a reservation for you this evening?"

"Yes, that would be under Bridger Goins." Bridger looked to Brooke, who smiled at his ingenuity in making a reservation while she was getting ready.

"Excellent. I see here you have requested a table for two looking over the canal. I have just the spot for you. Geta will show you to your table and I will see that the server brings you a bottle of wine right away. Thank you for joining us this evening."

Brooke and Bridger followed Geta to the table. She was about Brooke's age, a petite handful of smiles. She lingered at the table, answering their questions about the hotel, the neighborhood, and herself. She had graduated from college, but could not find a full-time job in her field of museum science. She apprenticed during the day at a local museum to get experience and advance her name in the industry. Those who earned prestigious positions, like the ones Geta sought, kept them until retirement.

Cobalt blue and silver velvet drapes framed the fifteen-foot windows. Night had fallen, and colored lights reflected in the canal. Huge ornate crystal chandeliers dotted the room. Amber candle flames flickered in contrast to the black linen tablecloths. Wait staff, dressed in formal uniforms, moved through the restaurant with precision and confidence.

The sommelier brought wines to taste and made pairing recommendations.

"I'm having the stuffed pike but I'm not fond of white wines. Could you recommend a red, or perhaps a blush?" Brooke had her favorite wines at home; she preferred a semi-dry red wine.

The sommelier, Harch, poured a full-bodied cabernet for her to taste. "We are not so snooty here that we limit our fish pairings to whites only. I would never tell anyway. I'm like a hair specialist. You can tell me anything." He winked at the pair. He was mature, knowledgeable and seemed to love his job and talking to guests. He checked on the couple throughout the evening.

Brooke enjoyed her meal. Bridger ordered wild Beemster duck stuffed with chanterelle mushrooms. They shared a cherry hangop dessert and a stroopwaffle parfait. To finish the meal, Harch served an after dinner liquor.

"Harch, you have been most attentive this evening. Thank you for your kind service." Bridger had watched Harch throughout the evening. The care he showed their table was the same as he showed others. He was constantly smiling and pulled wines from all areas of the cellar to bring the perfect bottle to each guest.

"You're such a delightful couple! It's been a pleasure to serve you. I hope the rest of your stay here at the hotel and in our fine city is enjoyable." He nodded and excused himself to attend to new patrons at a nearby table.

"It's so funny that everyone thinks we're a couple. I must admit, it has been easy hanging with you today. Thank you for asking me to join you for such a fine meal."

"You are most welcome, Bridger. I agree, it's been a wonderful day. But it's not over." Brooke looked at her watch. "According to my watch, it's karaoke time!"

She smiled as she pulled the napkin off her lap and laid it on the table. "Unless you're too chicken."

Bridger stood quickly. He swiftly caught his napkin before it fell from his lap.

"What did you call me?" He jokingly teased back. He held his arm out for Brooke to take. "Let's take this party to the top floor and see what they've got."

THE EPIC LOUNGE was dark with twinkle lights and mirrors providing ambient lighting. A young man in tight jeans and a Ramones t-shirt was moving around the room with a microphone, singing something reminiscent of a Michael Jackson tune, but Brooke couldn't place it. There was a decent crowd for 8:30.

Brooke and Bridger found two open seats near the center of the room and ordered water and sodas. They watched tables of locals pass the microphone around. With several ales already under their belt, they were having fun. In this room, the crowd was intimate. Instead of signing up to sing a song, they passed the microphone to another table with each new tune.

As the microphone came closer to their table, Bridger felt more and more anxious. He tried to distract himself with conversation.

Brooke knew this would be a test of character for her. He was intimidated and had to really stretch his comfort zone to join her.

Brooke reached for the microphone from the nearby table as soon as she heard the introduction to Madonna's *Papa Don't Preach*. A song by a female artist meant, in her mind, that Bridger wouldn't have to sing. She stood and moved through the audience, passing Bridger's chair early in her performance. She invited some women to join her as she moved around the room and winked at the guys, or stroked their cheek. She knew how to work the crowd and looked right at home with the mic in her hands.

Bridger's mouth dropped when Brooke started singing. What a woman! She was beautiful, kind, bright, interesting... and she could sing! His mother would love Brooke. When she finished, she got a tipsy standing ovation from the crowd and a kiss on the cheek from her tablemate. "Wow! You were amazing. So that's how your choir sings, eh?"

Brooke smiled. "Not usually, but some might say we are racy at times."

It was nearly midnight when Bridger and Brooke found themselves back in the lobby lounge. Neither of them wanted to end what turned out to be an incredible day. Neither of them had been looking to meet someone on their vacation. Both of them were glad they had, but had no vision of anything more than a chance meeting in a foreign city.

"Bridger, I hate to say it, but I'm beat. I think jet lag is finally catching up with me. I can barely keep my eyes open and it's not because of the company." Brooke shifted on the lounger they were sitting on. She wanted to stand up and walk to the elevator, but at the same time she did not want the night to end.

"I understand completely. I've kept you out too late already. I've had a surprising and fun day and evening with you, Brooke. Never in my wildest dreams could I have envisioned this day when I left the base. I need you to know that under different circumstances, I would ask to see you again and again."

Brooke stood. "That is so sweet of you to say. It has been the best day ever. I think the most we can hope for, for now, is to stay in touch from a distance. Who knows what the future may bring? I wish for you all the best and brilliant fun while you continue your career and your travels. I can honestly say you have opened a spot in my heart and I will carry you with me into the future. That's saying a lot from someone who rarely has time for the flowery side of life."

Bridger faced Brooke and looked deeply into her eyes. "Dearest Brooke, you have touched my soul. For now, I bid you a good night and a hearty thank you for a day well spent. If you need anything while traveling in Germany, please, promise me you'll reach out to me."

Bridger raised her hand to his mouth and delivered the gentlest of kisses to it. He pressed a piece of paper with his telephone number into her palm as he lowered her hand. With a sweet tear brimming at the corner of her eye, Brooke smiled and nodded, then turned toward the elevator and slowly walked away. Bridger watched as his fun-loving partner for the day slipped into the night, behind the metal doors of the elevator and back to her life. He graciously returned the borrowed dinner jacket and said farewell to the lobby staff before leaving. He sat in the parking lot in his beat-up BMW and looked up at the stately hotel, wondering which room Brooke was in and if she was looking out the window thinking of him.

Brooke was looking out onto the parking lot. She spotted Bridger's car and watched for it to drive away. Maybe the battery died, and he was waiting for help. His words rang in her head. What did it mean to touch someone's soul? The kiss to her hand was so sweet and so gentle. She wondered what it would have been like to embrace him and press their lips together. Brooke imaged sweetness, contentment and a thrill all rolled up together. As she stood there daydreaming, the BMW headlights burst on and the little car slowly crept out of the parking lot, as reluctant to leave as the driver.

7

Brooke woke when the early morning light streamed through the drapes, left open just a few hours earlier when she watched magical moments fade into the night. Her sleep, although short, was peaceful and refreshing. Her parents would arrive in Frankfurt in the early afternoon. She couldn't dally long in the hotel before making the four-and-a-half hour drive.

Brooke stepped into a pair of stylish jeans and loafers, put on a sweater and ran the brush through her hair before tying it back. She brushed on mascara, ran lip-gloss over her curvy lips and tossed the last of her toiletries into the bag. She wheeled her suitcase to the doorway of the room, turned toward the window and took in a deep breath. Yesterday was the best day ever, and she planned to carry the high with her throughout the rest of the trip.

At the lobby desk another sweet attendant in carefully pressed clothing checked her out. When told that she didn't have time for a sit-down meal, the attendant handed over a boxed breakfast. "Compliments of the hotel, miss. We hope your stay exceeded your expectations."

"You have no idea," she smiled. "It was fantastic! I even sang karaoke."

"Oh, what fun! The Epic Lounge is very popular with the locals. I hope they weren't too rowdy for you."

"They were all having a splendid time, so we just joined in, minus the alcohol."

"That's terrific! Is there anything more I can do for you before you depart? Do you need a map or anything?"

"Actually, if you just point me toward Frankfurt, I'll be good to go. You have all been so kind and accommodating. Next time, I will plan to stay longer."

Politely declining the bellman's offer of help, Brooke picked up the page of driving directions printed by the desk attendant and her bags. She walked through the grand entrance back to the parking lot, where she paused to look at the empty space where the old, rusted, crinkled BMW had rested the evening before.

"Until next time..." she whispered into the crisp air, her heated breath carrying the words away.

With bags loaded and the directions on the seat beside her, she steered the car toward Frankfurt. After an hour or so on the road, she took her first rest stop. She found a roadside gas station with snacks, grabbed a bottle of juice and a large coffee. She was making good time and wouldn't stop again until she fueled up near the airport in Frankfurt. The plan was to arrive at the airport about the same time her parents' plane was scheduled to land. They had to go through baggage claim and customs before she would see them.

Brooke got to the airport as planned, but her parents' plane was about fifteen minutes behind schedule. There was plenty of time to go inside, grab a cup of coffee and nearly doze off as she sat in the waiting area. She pulled out her phone and turned it on. A smile spread across her face as she looked down at the screen. *Still floating here and WOW, can you sing! Thanks again for a great time. B.*

A crowd was exiting the customs area. She quickly turned the phone off and stowed it in her purse, planning to return the message later. After gulping down the last of the lukewarm coffee, she walked to the exit archway where her parents would soon emerge.

LINDA AND FRANK walked hand in hand down the jetway toward the exit. Linda said goodbye to another passenger. A flight attendant rushing by turned to say something to Linda and Frank before hurrying on her way. It seemed that Linda and Frank had made new friends on the flight. Linda was the outgoing one. She never met a stranger... a trait that had embarrassed Brooke on more than one occasion.

"Hello! Hello!" Linda waved vigorously when she spotted Brooke. Brooke smiled and waved back. It was time for her to switch gears to being the entertainer. She was grateful to have read up on the various attractions they planned to see.

Linda walked quicker as she approached the exit sign, dragging Frank with her. She greeted Brooke with a big bear hug. "How was the Concorde? I bet it was delightful. And Amsterdam? How did you find the city? Did you get to do everything you wanted?"

"Hi Mom... Dad. There's plenty of time for a report in the car. I want to know - how was your flight? Any problems?" While helping with the luggage, Brooke began walking, leading them to the parked rental car.

"Your dad took us to the wrong gate in New York, but other than nearly missing our connection, there were no problems." Linda poked Frank in the ribs gently with her elbow.

"If that's the way you remember it, I guess that's the way it went." Frank had been Linda's scapegoat for forty years. It was a running joke in the family.

"Okay, so I may need my eyes checked. I swear that S1 looked like S51."

"Wow, Mom! That's quite a spread. You must have backtracked two miles."

"Yep, it was a great workout. By the time we made it to the right gate we were both worn out. It helped us nap to pass the time on the flight. We didn't have that quick flight you enjoyed."

"It looked like you must have visited some on the plane, too. I saw you talking to the crew and passengers when you came out of the gate."

"You know your mother. She's always making new friends."

"Yes, and I don't intend to stop now. They were delightful and I got some great ideas of things to take home as souvenirs. I might even find a wedding present for Lana and Pablo."

"Here we are. Let me open the trunk for your luggage. Do you need to pull anything out right now? By the time we get to the hotel we should be able to check in."

"Not me. I'm good." Frank was low maintenance. It took little more than being around his family to fulfill his needs.

"If we will do much walking I might want my other walking shoes. You know, the foot doctor told me it was a good idea to switch my shoes during the day to keep my bunions from burning." Linda was higher maintenance than her husband.

"I don't think we will walk much before we check into the hotel. Let's head that way now and see if we can check in. If there isn't a room ready yet we can grab some lunch. You probably had something on the plane, but I have had nothing but coffee and juice since I left Amsterdam."

"That sounds great to me. I think the time change is making me hungry." Frank had a hearty appetite. He rarely bothered to make up an excuse to eat.

The rooms were ready to check into by the time they arrived at the hotel. They spent some time freshening up and unpacking a little before regrouping in the lobby for lunch and exploration. Brooke had detailed notes from hours of studying the guidebooks. She sketched out a walking tour.

The walk took them into the Old Town district with cobbled streets and medieval timber framed buildings. As they walked, Brooke pointed out some of the historical sites she learned about from the guidebooks. She described international trades, a marketplace filled with artisans' crafts and meeting places of political leaders of the time.

Brooke stopped in front of an old cathedral, lit beautifully against the fading brilliant blue sky. She described the coronation ceremonies that took place there centuries before. Pointing toward the Coronation Route, she described some of the coronation rituals and ceremonies. She shared what she knew about Charlemagne, the founding father of Frankfurt, as well as other notable kings and emperors.

The lanes were dotted with homes of famous poets, composers and philosophers. Brooke shared stories she'd read of colorful characters, and some elusive ones as well, that made Old Town Frankfurt a center of culture, intrigue and rich history dating back to Roman times.

By early evening, they had seen the most desired sights and were ready to return to the hotel to wind down with a small meal and a drink. Their hotel was near old town, where there were several restaurants to choose from. They decided on a nearby apple-wine pub for a light dinner.

"Well, honey, this is already a glorious trip. I had just a delightful time looking around this afternoon. Can you believe all the wooden toys and ornaments? I was tempted to pick up several things but it just seems so early in the trip." Linda had a knack for finding just the right gift for friends and family. She had already purchased some honey and lavender sachets while walking through the marketplace.

Linda stretched her arm across the table and handed Brooke a package. "Here! I know you probably won't buy anything for yourself, so I got you this lovely handmade lavender soap. Just smell it. It's so fresh."

Brooke took the soap and brought it up to her nose. It smelled like the dozen others she had tested herself.

"It's lovely, Mom. Thank you. Now, shall we talk about tomorrow? I was thinking we could meet for breakfast early, check out and start our drive to Munich. Dad, will it be okay with you if we stop in Stuttgart to tour the Mercedes-Benz Museum?"

"That would be terrific! Let's do it."

"And Mom, I know you love flowers." Brooke handed over a travel book open to a certain page. "Here's the Whilhelma Zoological-Botanical Gardens. How about if we stop there and explore the grounds?"

"Oh, wow!" Linda looked at the page in the book. "I see they have a zoo, too. This is really special, Brooke. Thanks for scouting it out for us. I wonder if I might find some exotic flowers Lana could use for her wedding."

There it was. The wedding talk was starting already.

"I have another surprise for you later in the day, in Munich, so we can't loiter too long on the way. And we will have to get an early start. I hope you don't mind."

"Mind? Of course not! We can sleep when we're dead. Your mother and I appreciate all you've done to put this trip together, Brooke."

"You are welcome. The restaurant is open for European breakfast buffet at 6:30. Shall we plan to meet then? You guys can nap in the car if you need to on the way tomorrow."

"There will be no napping, I guarantee it! Your dad and I don't want to miss a thing."

"That sounds like an excellent plan. We will be ready to go whenever you say so. Do we need to gas up the car before we take off in the morning?"

"No, I took care of that before I picked you up at the airport. I am looking forward to the drive and the stop in Stuttgart. I chatted with someone in Amsterdam who was familiar with the area we are going to and he said it was all interesting."

"Really? Was he a tourist too?"

"Not exactly. He's stationed here with the U.S. Army. He tries to bundle his days off and tours around in an old BMW he picked up."

"Sounds like an interesting fella you met."

"Yes, he is. It was a reassuring chance meeting. It's nice to know there are still genuine nice guys out there."

"Is he available?"

"Mom! He lives in Germany and has no immediate plans to return to the States. But, yes, he is available."

"Well honey, you'll meet your Pablo one day." Linda wanted her daughter's life to be perfect, and in her mind that required a husband to round out the picture. There was security in having a man around to take care of things and pay the bills. Brooke had not adopted her mother's philosophy, but navigated around the subject, avoiding landmines whenever possible. She should have kept Bridger to herself. Sharing what little she did just opened up a slippery can of worms.

That was a conversation stopper. Brooke was not the least bit interested in meeting a 'Pablo', whatever that was. She enjoyed meeting and spending time with Bridger. She couldn't see herself turning her life upside down to be with him though. It wasn't in the cards for her.

All the talk of Bridger reminded Brooke that she hadn't responded to his text. It already seemed like days, instead of hours, since she saw him. Exhaustion from the thrilling, busy first few days of travel hit when she returned to her hotel room for an early night. Before crawling into bed, she sent off a text message and turned the phone off. *Had a fantastic time! Stay well. B.* It was anticlimactic, but all Brooke could manage in her exhausted state. Still, she fell asleep with a smile, reflecting on their chance meeting.

8

$\mathcal{B}$rooke was wide awake by four a.m. She brewed a cup of coffee in her room, added the complimentary packet of raw sugar, and opened the drapes. As she sat in the deep purple velour easy chair in front of the window, the lights of the Frankfurt skyline and the Sachsenhausen Main riverbank danced before her. Thoughts of Bridger came in the silence. Was there some purpose for their chance meeting that she was ignoring?

Brooke's thoughts drifted to the office and her expected promotion. She recalled some documents that should be included in her application, when Jeff's position opens. She made a mental note to call Monica tonight before going to bed in Munich.

By six o'clock Brooke had checked out of her beautiful hotel room and was drinking coffee in the lobby. At six-thirty on the dot, Frank and Linda exited the elevator with luggage in tow. The threesome enjoyed a hearty European breakfast with baskets full of pastries and dense whole-grain breads, trays of fresh grass-fed butter, and jams, fish pickled and canned with different sauces, a variety of eggs, fresh fruits and muesli with local yogurt. They each sampled several items, sharing their impression of new flavors.

By eight o'clock they were in the rental car headed for Stuttgard, then Munich. As they were making excellent time,

50

Brooke surprised her parents with a quick stop to view Heidelberg Castle. They did not tour the castle interior, but walked the grounds, took loads of pictures, and studied the structures. The variety of architectural styles used over the 400-year building period fascinated Frank.

Linda was less fascinated with the massive red stone structure, but the gardens piqued her interest. It was not prime growing season, but she could envision the beauty of the gardens with their geometric plantings, statues, pergolas, pavilions and water features.

"Wouldn't this be the most romantic place for a wedding? There's a phenomenal backdrop from every angle." Linda moved through the garden, her hands held in front of her framing the various views as if she was taking photos.

"Sure, Mom, but I don't know if they allow weddings here." Brooke was desperately hoping every day of their vacation was not filled with talk of weddings.

"Look Brooke! Just look at this courtyard over here behind this garden! Great for the reception! Just imagine long tables set up in a horseshoe shape, a huge centerpiece on a tabletop in the middle, tables covered with linens and draped with flowers, china and crystal. Oh, yes. I can see it now."

"Mom, are you planning to marry Dad again? I mean, why are you talking about weddings?"

"You know I'm a romantic at heart. Since Lana announced her plans, I just can't turn off the wedding planner in my head. She's on autopilot. Just let me create, will ya? I mean nothing by it; it's just fun for me."

"Okay, if that's what works for you. I'll just stand back and let you have your fun."

"Thanks, Brooke. I mean no harm."

"Well, I hope you're taking pictures and making notes so you can recreate these images one day."

"That's a brilliant idea. I hadn't thought of writing it down, but I am taking pictures."

"Here, put this brochure with your things. You can make notes right on here. It will help jog your memory when you get back home and relive this vacation." Brooke handed Linda a marketing brochure that she had picked up at the castle entrance. As she thought more about it, Brooke realized that if the castle was not marketing weddings they were missing a tremendous opportunity to capitalize on the beauty and uniqueness of the castle. After all, what bride wouldn't at least contemplate a fairytale wedding?

AFTER AN HOUR of gawking at the castle, the trio climbed back into the car to continue the trip to Stuttgart. They drove along the Neckar River and observed the castles and terraced vineyards from a distance. There was no time to stop today. Brooke made a mental note that she wanted to visit this valley with its mixture of Baroque castles, fairytale skylines, and open fields. To Brooke, this place oozed the feel of romance that one could bathe in.

Stuttgart was a bustling place - more modern and metropolitan than what they saw earlier in the day. Brooke had pre-arranged a personal guided tour for the family at the Mercedes-Benz Museum. Paul, their guide, easily extracted from Frank the vehicles and eras he was most interested in. The ninety-minute tour flew by. They had covered most of the 16,000 square foot museum. Even Linda was entertained.

"Paul, thank you for sharing your wealth of knowledge and entertaining us on this tour. I can't believe it's over already. I learned so much and I am so impressed with what the museum has to offer."

"You are welcome, Frank." Paul turned to Linda. "I hope you and Brooke also enjoyed it."

"Oh yes! It was wonderful even for me," she gushed.

Frank reached his hand out to bid Paul farewell. "I certainly did. You're a wonderful guide and if there's a place for me to give my review, I'm happy to do that."

"That will probably come to my email, Dad. I will share it with you so you can give your review. Now Paul, if you will just point us to the bistro please. We'll pick up a box lunch and coffee and be on our way. We are visiting Whilhelma Zoological-Botanical Gardens. We need to get to Munich yet today."

"Ja, sure. The bistro is right around that corner there." Paul pointed just past the elevators and to the right. "You will barely have time to gobble your lunch before you get to the gardens. It's only about 10 minutes from here. Then, in no less than three hours, you should arrive in Munich. Do you need a map? I can print one for you, if you do."

"No, that's okay. I have a great guidebook in the car that has maps. We should make our destination just fine. Thank you again, Paul." Brooke reached out to shake Paul's hand and give him a tip for his fine work. She was happy to see both her parents engaged in the tour.

They chose brioche, potted meat sandwiches and lattes from the bistro, then loaded back into the rental car and drove to the gardens. Despite it being off-season, Linda was thoroughly entertained with the plant houses where tropical plants and birds and desert plants showed off their beauty. Plants over a hundred years old stood amongst them. Stunning camellias, in hues ranging from white to pink to deep red, graced their glass house.

They rushed through the zoo, stopping only to interact with the gorillas. Brooke hurried her parents through the garden patios and around the hedges back to the car. "I told you there is another surprise for you in Munich. If we go now, I think we can make it."

BROOKE WORRIED A BIT. By her rough calculations, they had four hours to find their hotel, check in, change and get to the opera house. Maybe she had tried to squeeze too much into this, their first full day of exploring Germany. They passed many sites of interest on their way to Munich - the English Garden, Dachau Concentration Camp, and others. These would have to wait for now; there would be scheduled time in their agenda for day trips during the week ahead when they could visit properly.

During the car ride, Linda made notes in the margins of brochures, noting her ideas, findings and feelings. When she spoke, she was animated and excited over all the things they had already seen on this trip. "Frank, I hope you're getting some good shots with that camera. You haven't used it in a long time, but I'm sure you've still got the best trigger finger in Kansas."

"I think I'm doing ok. I just scrolled through them and erased a few..."

"Are you sure you want to erase them already? Shouldn't we look at them together to be sure?"

"Linda, trust me on this. They were blurry or thumb shots. There was nothing salvageable in them and we need to make room on the little chip thingy that holds the digital images."

"Okay, honey. I'll trust you. I snapped a couple photos with my camera, too, for a little security."

Brooke navigated the Autobahn well; they made it to the outskirts of Munich with ample time to spare. However, she had not anticipated the slow traffic they encountered once in the city, that ate up precious time. Besides the traffic, the directions to the hotel did not take into account changes to the roads and construction in the two years since the book was published. Brooke found herself going in circles, unable to get to the area of town where the hotel was. Since leaving the Autobahn, they had not seen a service station to stop at and ask for directions. On the inside, she panicked and reprimanded herself for not being organized enough. Outwardly, she remained calm for her parents.

"I'm sorry, guys. I thought it would be more straightforward than this. We should have been there already."

After going through a roundabout, which she was sure she had traveled through twice already, Brooke pulled over to the side of the road. She was lost in a foreign country with her parents, feeling insecure and out of control – feelings she was not familiar with. She sat for a moment, silently going over her options before coming to a decision. Bridger's plea to be the one she called if in need rang in her ears and warmth rose through her core. Unsteady in a strange country, with confidence slightly shaken and help potentially just a call away, her usual fierce independence dissolved.

"I'm just going to call my new friend and see if he has any suggestions," she announced.

Brooke pulled out her phone, turned it on and dialed Bridger. It rang several times before she heard a panting, "Hello."

"Hey Bridger, it's Brooke."

"Oh my gosh, Brooke! I didn't even have time to look at the screen to see who was calling. Did you make it to Munich? I tried to catch you and surprise you in Frankfurt but you had just left the hotel when I got there. Unfortunately, there is a temporary reintroduction of border control and I got stuck in the middle of it."

"Oh, no! I can't believe the timing!"

"Me either. It's quite a story and I will tell you sometime, but hey, you called me. What's up?"

"I'm here with my folks and I'm trying desperately to get to our hotel so we can get to our event for this evening. My guide-book is outdated, and at this rate I don't think we will make it." She explained where they were and where they needed to be.

"Tell you what. I'm about ready to leave work. I think I know where you are, but I don't know exactly how to get you to your hotel. But if you're too late for your event already, and you don't mind waiting for me about twenty minutes, I can help you out of your jam."

Brooke looked at her mom and dad. They were getting only bits and pieces of the conversation, but enough to know plans were changing.

"You know, we can do that. We can try to get tickets for the Bayerische Staatsoper Opera House another night." Her dad, in the passenger's seat, gave a sneaky thumbs-up that Linda couldn't see. Brooke relaxed and laughed. "Okay. We'll be waiting here in the rental car."

"And I'll be in my beat up BMW! Keep your phone on in case I can't find you. See you soon."

She hung up and turned to her mother. "Well, the cat's out of the bag. I know you said you would like to experience the opera, so I got tickets for us all. As you heard, we will not make it."

"Oh, honey, that was so sweet of you." Linda's tone changed quickly. "I say, let's take this Bridger friend of yours out for dinner instead and get the scoop from him. How long has he been stationed here?"

"He's been here about six months. He's explored a fair amount and probably has loads of things to tell us about. I'm sure he would appreciate dinner out, but we'll have to check with him before we plan on it."

Frank reached his long arm across the front seat and rested his huge hand on his daughter's shoulder. "This one little hiccough will not ruin our trip. In fact, I think everything works out exactly how it's supposed to. Now, let's have a pleasant evening anyway, shall we?"

He looked back over the car seat toward his wife, who was oblivious to the pep talk meant at least partially for her. She was engrossed in a travel book, looking at day trips from Munich.

9

$\mathcal{A}$n hour later, the four stood in the lobby of the hotel. Bridger looked extremely polite and proper in uniform.

"Bridger, we can't thank you enough for coming to our rescue. Brooke's a great driver, but when the directions are wrong there's no place to go. And she is such a determined independent person, I swear, she did thirty circles before we stopped." Brooke bristled at the comment and shook it off. Her mother knew her well.

"You're welcome, Linda. That has happened to me before. With all the roundabouts and unannounced traffic flow changes, the roads do not match the books. I'm glad it worked out so that I could help."

"We would like to thank you properly. Do you care to join us for dinner? We'll find some nice place around here and check out the local fare."

"Thanks, Frank. If it's all right with Brooke, I would love to join you. It's always nice to visit with Americans and get caught up on life there. I can give my buddy a call and get his recommendation for a good place. He's a real foodie and knows all the best places to go."

"I'm grateful for yet another rescue from you," Brooke smiled. "I haven't even told Mom and Dad about our crazy first meeting."

"Well, that sounds like great dinner conversation. How about if you all get checked in and I'll scope out the restaurants? We can reconvene down here in about twenty minutes, if that's enough time for you all."

The trio agreed they could be ready. It was enough time for Brooke to change clothes, wash her face and reapply light make-up. Frank changed his shirt, and Linda looked fresh as a daisy when they reassembled.

"You are a bunch of quick change artists!"

Brooke stared at Bridger in amazement. "Well, look at you! Out of uniform and everything!"

"I try to always carry a change of clothes. Never know what might come up."

"You look great! Did you learn anything about the local cuisine?" Brooke had tucked a travel book in her purse just in case they needed an extra resource.

"My buddy recommends a place just a few blocks from here. They have traditional Schnitzel. Serve it up with beer and a side of cucumber salad and you will eat like the locals."

"That sounds great to me! Which way do we go?" Frank loved to eat, and meat was his mainstay. He was hungry!

Bridger led them out the door and down the street. It was early evening, and dusk was fading to night.

"I see all these decorations hanging on poles lining the streets. Is there a special event coming up?" Linda noticed everything. Each town they passed through had flags, but no two towns had the same flags.

"There are always flags. Sometimes they are for special holidays, but often they are just what's flying today. You are here now between Oktoberfest and the opening of Christmas Market. These, to the best of my knowledge, are just decorative and not related to any specific celebration."

"Well, I think they are lovely. Frank, honey, you got a picture of them, didn't you?"

"Yes, I got several pics for you. I'm not sure what you will do with all these pictures, but you'll have plenty to choose from."

"That sounds like a familiar problem. I've got a load of photos and SD cards with digital images. Someday I will make something of them, I'm not sure what. But for now, I wait until I have a bundle and send them home to my mom to put in safekeeping for me."

"Oh, that's nice. Where is your mom?"

"Here's the restaurant. After you." Bridger motioned for the women, then Frank, to enter the noisy pub.

A hostess in a blue and white gingham Bavarian-style dress greeted them. Her long blonde braids and bubbly personality were perfect for the role. Later they learned that she was working her way through University and studying to be a nurse.

They sat at a large wooden table with wooden benches on along each side.

"I love this!" Linda smiled at the group. "What a lively place."

It was noisier than expected which made conversation difficult. Bridger leaned over to Brooke, who sat beside him. "Is this too noisy?"

She looked up at him and smiled. "I think it's just perfect."

He smiled back.

"Linda, you asked where my mom lives. She's outside Chicago in a tiny town called Hampshire."

"And your father?"

"He passed a few years ago. Victim of a drunk driver, I'm afraid."

"Oh, I'm so sorry." Linda reached across and patted his hand.

"Thank you. He was a brilliant man and I miss him, but I am grateful for the time we had him."

"Was he also in the service?"

"No. He was not accepted into the service because of a congenital malformation that affected his hearing." In anticipation of the continuing inquiries by Linda, Bridger continued. "He worked with his father in the local hardware store and eventually took it over. He and Mom were very active in the community and Mom continues to serve on several small committees. It's not a heavily populated area, but the community is active."

"Okay Mom. That's enough third degree for Bridger. Have

you all decided what you're ordering?" Brooke looked apologetically at Bridger while she picked up her cold beer.

Linda started telling them what her choice was when the waitress arrived to take their orders. Two of them ordered the Schnitzel while the other two ordered roasted pork knuckle with red cabbage and dumplings.

They were on their second round of cold beers when the waitress brought the food. Linda's eyes grew big when her knuckle was served. "Oh, my! Look at this enormous plate! There is no way I can eat all this."

The waitress laughed. "You will do better than you think. There's a lot of bone in there. Enjoy!"

Linda was the first to try her food. "The crackling is to die for. Frank, honey, you have to try this." Linda cut a slice of her pork and slid it onto his plate.

"That's fine, but this Schnitzel is bigger than my plate. I've never seen such a gigantic piece of meat." He shared a portion of his meat with Linda.

Bridger remembered having the same reaction the first time he saw these famous Bavarian meals. "Can you believe the size of these portions? They eat well here in Germany. These two dishes are typically the most overwhelming when it comes to size. That Schnitzel is nearly paper-thin. It's a regular-sized piece of meat that's pounded very thin."

"Hey, there's another food you want to try while you're here. I learned of this great family-style restaurant that serves Weisswurst. White sausages with sweet mustard, a handmade pretzel and beer are about as authentic as you can get around here and this place has them in spades. They also have the occasional minstrel group that comes through and plays local music."

"That sounds great!" Brooke pulled out her travel guide and handed it to Bridger. "If you don't mind, can you mark the restaurant in here? I know I won't remember the name otherwise."

"Sure." Bridger took the book and between bites found the restaurant and placed a strip of paper between the pages.

"So Bridger, when did you get back to Munich? Brooke said

you met in Amsterdam. Was that a vacation for you or were you on a mission?" Linda knew nothing about the U.S. forces overseas or what type of work Bridger would be doing. Her point of reference was movies.

Bridger looked at Brooke. "I started to tell you about coming back." Brooke nodded.

"I took a couple of days leave just so I could explore. I like to do that when I'm on assignment in a foreign location. It keeps the travel and time away from home more interesting for me. The trip to Amsterdam was a quick trip to hit the highlights. I would love to go back and spend more time there. It's a very friendly place to visit." Brooke and Bridger locked eyes, each remembering an element of their time together in Amsterdam.

"But I knew you were all coming here and I wanted to meet you, so I came back early."

Brooke's knitted her eyebrows together, slightly annoyed with his forwardness yet flattered with his intent.

"I was hoping to catch up with you in Frankfurt. I had just spent a couple of days there and could have shared some insights with you. But they stood up border control for some reason. They stopped me and searched my vehicle. You've seen my old BMW. Maybe they thought I was a drug runner or something. Anyway, by the time I got to your hotel, you had already checked out. It sounds like you had a great stay and saw a few sights."

"Yeah, it was a wonderful day. Brooke is a superb guide and travel partner. She has single-handedly put this package together after researching for months. If the rest of the trip is even half as fantastic as yesterday and today, she will get gold stars all the way around."

"Thanks Mom. Provided we don't get lost too many times again. I'll have to improve on that!"

"Well, I am sorry you had to miss the opera tonight. Maybe you can try for tomorrow night?"

Frank looked at Bridger and gently shook his head. He did not want to pursue tickets for the opera.

"I'll look into it." Brooke looked at her dad and winked.

. . .

THE GROUP FINISHED dinner and slowly walked back to the hotel, studying the shop windows along the way. Frank and Linda set the pace. Brooke and Bridger walked side-by-side behind them, occasionally bumping up against one another. They were as comfortable together as they had been when they first met.

Brooke reminded herself that Bridger lived in Germany and she lived on a different continent, far from the life he had chosen. She was not interested in a long distance relationship. But if she was looking for a partner, Bridger had at least the top fifty qualities she was looking for. She was lost in her own thoughts when they reached the hotel lobby.

"Well, kids, I'm pooped. I'm heading up to bed." Frank reached his hand out. "Bridger, it's been wonderful to meet you. Thank you for joining us tonight and for sharing your wealth of knowledge of the area. It's been a real treat and I hope we get to see you again before we leave town."

Bridger smiled as he shook Frank's hand. "Thank you, sir. I hope to see you again, too."

Linda rushed in with a hug. "I'm sure your momma would give you an enormous momma bear hug if she were here so since she's not, I'm going to do it."

"Uh, well, thank you ma'am. You are right. My momma would definitely give me a big hug and remind me to brush my teeth. It's a funny ritual we've had for many years now."

"Has she been over to visit you?"

"Not yet, but I'm giving her a ticket for Christmas." Bridger held his finger to his lips. "Shhhh, don't tell her."

The group laughed.

"What a wonderful son you are! Thanks again, Bridger. Hope to see you tomorrow." With that, Linda turned, took Frank by the arm and led him to the elevator. She turned and said over her shoulder, "I've got to get my chaperone to bed before he turns into a pumpkin."

Brooke and Bridger watched them get on the elevator and disappear into the night.

"Your parents are wonderful. It was a real treat to meet them."

"They are pretty great. I'm glad you were able to join us. And help us!"

They stood a short while longer in silence.

"I'm a little wired. Would you like to hang out a bit?" Bridger looked around and pointed to a sign showing the hotel lounge in the lobby's corner. "How about a nightcap or a coffee over there?"

"Sure, that sounds great."

NEARLY TWO HOURS LATER, Brooke checked her watch. If she hurried to her room, she could still reach Monica at the office. She didn't want Bridger to know she was going back to her room to work. That seemed like a rude message to send him, after he had been so generous with his time. "Bridger, I've just hit a wall. I need to get some sleep. How does tomorrow look for you? Any chance you can join us for some of those white sausages?"

"I would love to join you. Barring any unforeseen issues, I could meet you by five. Just text me and let me know where you are and I'll come find you." The glint in Bridger's eyes and the grin on his face said all Brooke needed to hear. He was excited to spend time with her. As strongly as she willed it, she wasn't able to overcome the fluttering feeling within; she was more than happy to spend time with him too. She told herself it would pass and soon this would all be a happy memory. For now, she would enjoy it.

Brooke walked Bridger out the front door of the hotel and said good night. They embraced in the glow of golden light coming from the orbs mounted beside the entrance. As much as they each wanted to seal the evening with a kiss, neither would take the risk. Hearts were at stake.

With a full heart, Brooke climbed into the elevator and ascended to her room.

10

---

lone in her hotel room, Brooke's thoughts quickly turned to her job. She felt a near panic wondering what the status of job openings was, and if she had put together a strong enough application package.

She thought briefly about the cost of calling the office. It was worth every cent to learn the gossip and set her application up for success, should there be an opening.

"Good afternoon. This is Monica. How may I help you?" They didn't have the best connection on their long distance call. There were times when voices faded, there were delays and sometimes they seemed to talk simultaneously.

"Hello Monica. It's Brooke."

"Oh, Brooke! Sorry, I didn't see your number on the screen; I was just leaving to get to my daughter's school play. Is there something I can do for you real quick?"

"I was just checking to see if the job opening came up and if you know anything I should know. I mean, what's the gossip?"

Monica rolled her eyes and checked her watch. "It's really not..."

"Did they announce Jeff's retirement? Have they posted his job?"

"Really, Brooke. I have to…"

"I came up with more exemplars I need to put in my application package. Do you have a pen? Look under the Barber and Sons file and pull up that project plan. That's the best…"

"Brooke, I…"

"…one I've ever done and that should be included. I can text you a little intro you can put with it. And then in the Crosby file, you remember those elegant gardens we designed to enhance that ugly landscape they had? Well, I want to highlight those so be sure you print those files in color and make a special section in the packet."

Brooke added five new files to her application packet, each with introductions and dividers, for a job that wasn't even posted yet and may never be. Monica knew how important this was for Brooke, and it meant a promotion for her as well. She tossed her coat on the desk and furiously took notes as Brooke, whose voice echoed over the phone, dictated. Twenty minutes later, when the conversation was over, Monica was in tears. She was late for the performance and so angry with Brooke she could spit.

With red weepy eyes, she rushed past Hal on the way out of the office. He let her go, given the rush she seemed to be in, but made a note to follow up with her the following day.

RELIEVED that she had reached Monica and downloaded her thoughts before retiring for the night, Brooke turned her mind back to the evening with her parents and Bridger. Once again, time spent with Bridger was easy. Being with him was comfortable in a way she never knew before. They were in sync.

Brooke and her parents spent the following day sightseeing. Since they missed the opera and were unable to get new tickets, Brooke and Frank let Linda linger in the art museums of the Museum Embankment. They strolled through quirky shops and avoided the streets lined with big name department stores.

At lunchtime they found the restaurant that Bridger recommended for weisswurst. Linda and Frank wanted to wait for Bridger to join them for the special treat, but Brooke knew from her studies that this was not a meal to be enjoyed in the evening.

"These are wonderful! I'm so glad Bridger told us about this place." Linda dipped a slice of sausage in mustard and savored the flavor.

"Too bad your friend Bridger couldn't join us. This is fantastic. I would like to find a way to take a bunch of these home."

"I bet you can find them at home, Dad. There are enough Germans around Kansas; they probably make them somewhere. I would be tempted to take this tasty mustard home though."

It pleased Brooke that her parents liked Bridger. He wasn't a rancher, like her dad, but he was a well-rounded and interesting man. And handsome! Brooke knew she could be smitten if she allowed herself to be.

BRIDGER HAD PHONED Brooke early in the afternoon and asked if he could have the pleasure of taking them to dinner. He met the group in the hotel lobby precisely at five. "Hello all! How was everyone's day?"

Linda greeted Bridger with a hug. "We are great! Looking forward to the evening. How about yourself?"

Frank shook his hand. "Good to see you, Bridger."

"Yes, what is this surprise you have for us?" Brooke didn't really care. She looked forward to the evening no matter what the surprise, and knew they would have a wonderful time.

"Well if you're anything like me, when you travel you want to enjoy local cuisine. Is that right? I mean, if you want to eat Thai food, which I love, Germany is probably not the place you would do it."

"Oh, yes. We want authentic German food. My husband loves meat and potatoes and has not been disappointed yet. We trust you, Bridger. Let's do this."

"Okay. So here's the deal. I frequent this little teahouse in

Marienplatz Munich Old Town. Actually, it's a combination restaurant and teahouse. They have fabulous pastries and great stews at lunchtime. I try to go there at least a couple times a month. A few nights each month they take reservations for dinner. The menu is slim but the food is guaranteed to be authentic and fabulous. I took the liberty of making a reservation. Are you all game?"

"Yes, of course! It sounds fabulous."

"The other cool thing about this place is the owner will come out and tell everyone about the dishes offered, about the organic produce and meats they use and there will be a wine demonstration. The family has a small farm that sources much of their herbs and vegetables, meats, honey, fruits for pastries and jams… well, I had better not give it all away."

Brooke slid next to Bridger and put her arm in his. "Thank you Bridger. Let's get going then! Is this place within walking distance or do we need to drive there?"

"That's another fantastic thing. It's a bit of a walk, but after dinner you will want the digestive stroll home. I suggest, if everyone has their walking shoes on, that we head on over. We will walk through the city gates about a half-mile from here."

The women adjusted the wool scarves around their necks. Frank patted his pocket to confirm his wallet was in place.

"I'm looking forward to it Bridger. Now, tell us, what do you do to learn so much about places like this?" Linda found Bridger to be very engaging and a wonderful storyteller.

"I immerse myself into the community as early as I can. The best thing about my position here is that my schedule, unless I have to travel, is quite predictable so I can easily check schedules and see what's open. I love food and like to try new foods. I've found that even within a region, the locals can make one dish many ways depending on the cook."

"Well, that's true!" Brooke laughed. "Mom, you taught each of us girls to make chili and none of us makes it the same."

Linda took a slight detour down the chili tasting rabbit hole, and took over the conversation comparing the unique culinary style of each of her daughters. Bridger listened with amusement. Linda reminded him of his mother.

"Bridger, I don't think you ever told us if you have siblings."

"No, I don't think that came up before. I do. I have an older sister and a younger brother." In anticipation of further questions, he continued. "My sister is a dermatologist in the Twin Cities and my brother is a chef in Chicago."

"How fun is that! Does your brother specialize in any cuisine?"

"He does. He works at one of the top-end steak houses. It's part of a chain. He also has a business degree, and with that has had the opportunity to set up restaurants for this chain in other cities. He loves Chicago though and always comes home."

Bridger paused and pointed out some local fauna and remnants of medieval walls that once surrounded the city center. "Sometimes when you pass through the gate, it's like being transported back in time. That happens more commonly during the high tourist time. There are minstrels and Roman soldiers, peasant women carrying baskets of goods and mini parades with dignitaries and their followers. It can be a lot of fun."

The group paused when they passed through the gate to get their bearings.

"This place is crowded during the summer and Oktoberfest and Christmas season. Today we don't need to worry about getting separated from each other, but the central highlight of the square, and the meeting place for most tours and groups, is Marienplatz, or St. Mary's Square. You can see here, the Column of St. Mary and why it carries that name."

Bridger pointed to a large Roman column with a gold statute of the Virgin Mary on top.

"Oh, wow! I'm glad we waited to come here with you, Bridger. You just know so much. Isn't that beautiful? And rich with history, I bet. Frank, honey, get some pictures, please."

As they continued the walk to the restaurant, Bridger pointed out the Christmas Market location. The start of the market was several weeks away, but booths and attractions were already under construction.

"Oh, I think I need to come back for Christmas Market. I can already tell there is magic in the air when all these buildings are operational." Christmas was the one thing that softened Brooke's heart more than anything. She never lost the magical feeling of Christmas that she knew as a child. It remained a time when she celebrated her faith most boldly and stayed active with giving projects through church and her family, as well as work. She never passed an angel tree without taking a needy child's name, and then spent hours shopping for the perfect gift for that little stranger.

"That building over there is the New Town Hall. You've probably heard of a glockenspiel percussion instrument."

"We had one of those in high school band but I don't know if I've seen one since." Brooke lit up in anticipation of Bridger's explanation of glockenspiel.

"Here is Rathaus-Glockenspiel. You might want to come back tomorrow, between 11:00 and noon, and watch the display. Just up there…" Bridger pointed to the tower where colorful figures could be seen. "The story on the top floor depicts the very elaborate and festive marriage of Bavarian Duke Wilhelm V in the 1500s. He brought the first brewery to the city. There are jousters in that story as well, celebrating the blue Bavarians conquering the knight of Lothringen in red."

"I had no idea the Germans were such storytellers." Frank enjoyed this type of experience where they weren't just looking at things but learning about them as well. He definitely wanted to return to see this giant music box in action.

"On the second floor, the barrel makers do the Cooper's Dance. The story goes something like this. There was a plague and the Coopers, or barrel makers, used a dance with fancy footwork to lure the frightened people out of their homes at the end of the plague. I guess it was their way to get the economy going again. Anyway, after the dances are over, a golden bird pops out of the top of the glockenspiel."

"That is just awesome. I wish we could see it in action tonight. Thanks for telling us about it, Bridger." Linda reached out and put her arm around Bridger.

"There is a more simplistic show every evening at 9. We can come by here on our way out after dinner. If the timing is right, we will see an angel and a night watchman."

The group nodded in agreement.

"If you do come back tomorrow, I recommend you spend some time inside the glockenspiel building. From here, it looks like an old Gothic building that is sort of industrial and maybe abandoned. Once you get inside, you see incredible beauty. It's ornate, and if you go up to the observation deck you get an impressive view of the city. If the sky is clear, you can see the Alps."

Brooke looked at Linda. "Oh, we are definitely coming back tomorrow!"

"But, I thought we needed to head out of town to get to Nuremberg then on to Dresden and Berlin."

"We've got room to shuffle things around. If we come here after breakfast and check out, we can stay through the glockenspiel performance and then hit the road. We'll be okay. I'll study some tonight and have a plan. And I promise we won't get lost!"

"I've got some ideas, Brooke," Bridger added. "We can talk about them later. For now, I want to make sure you have the opportunity to look at the shops here. A few of them stay open into the evening. Let me know which ones you want to stop in and look around. We have about thirty minutes before our reservation and only ten minutes more to walk."

She liked the way her name rolled off Bridger's tongue. She also didn't mind him walking close to her and occasionally putting his hand on her shoulder or lower back to get her attention when pointing out some unique feature along the way.

Linda pulled Frank into a couple shops as they walked down the cobblestone pedestrian street, and picked up some trinkets to share with friends and family. They passed through a section of Old Town filled with pubs and restaurants. Cases of pastries and chocolates lined the windows, playful music piped into the air, and the cheerful chatter of pub patrons drifted out into the early evening.

Bridger paused. "This is it. We just go down these stairs into the basement."

"Huh. I would have missed this completely if you hadn't pointed out the stairs." Linda looked down into the stairwell. There were large windows at the basement level. She could see beautiful stained glass and vintage blown-glass light fixtures hanging throughout. "I can tell already that I will love this place."

Linda and Frank were the first to enter. The place was filled with antique dining tables and chairs, each with a unique style. Some were set with mismatched chairs, such as two with gold brocade seat covers, one with purple velvet and another with duck cloth floral. There were sideboards and hutches lined with exquisite antique tea services, trays, serving bowls and colored glasses. In another area there were vintage wine bottle storage lockers and shelves filled with colorful and ornate wine glasses of every size.

"Oh Bridger, this is magnificent! You are a man after my heart. I feel like I've just walked into the Sax of vintage ware." Linda loved the quality and beauty of old woods. Their home showcased several pieces that were passed down through the generations.

By the time they looked around and were seated, everyone was hungry. There was another round of gustatory delights from the group of fortuitous foodies. The menu had four fleshy main courses, so the group ordered one of everything to share, as well as the non-meat noodles stuffed with potatoes, spinach and curd.

Each enjoyed semolina dumplings and Munich coleslaw salad as starters. The shared main courses were a delicate carp with lemon curd sauce and greens, boiled beef with boiled potatoes and horseradish, braised pork with dumplings and cranberries and pink trout fillet with vegetables and spun potatoes.

They were too full to order dessert, but reserved the right to reconsider as they passed pastry shops on the way back to the hotel. The restaurant delivered (a gratis) a single apple cobbler for them to share, and insisted on providing each with an after dinner drink. The chef and staff spent a good deal of time with them. The atmosphere was intimate and, since the other patrons were mostly locals, the tourists got all the attention. As they left the cozy antique store restaurant, the chef shook hands with each of them and bid them a fine vacation.

They came upon the Glockenspiel just as the angel and night watchman were making their appearance. The night watchman emerged from the tower, blowing his horn.

"Locals refer to this performance as bedtime for the Bavarian child," Bridger explained. "The night watchman blows his horn three times, indicating curfew, and the angel floats out from the right with a hand held out over the head of the childlike monk known as Münchner Kindl. This figure is Munich's mascot. The angel is blessing the city. You can hear a Brahms tune in the background."

The group watched and listened for five minutes, and the show was over.

Frank enjoyed the show as much as any of them. "That was really neat. I read some about the mechanics behind all this and it's really well executed."

"That's right. It's very reliable. They also have a small selection of tunes they choose from and change up the music sometimes. I'm glad you liked it. As you can see, even the locals stop to enjoy it if they are in the area when it's playing."

By the time they reached the hotel, Frank and Linda were too tired to consider dessert or a chat. Knowing they were leaving the next day and would not see Bridger after tonight, they lingered in the lobby to say goodbye before heading up the elevator to bed.

"Bridger, son, it's been just so wonderful to meet you and enjoy your company these past couple of days. I'm not sure what stars were aligned or whatever when you and Brooke bumped into each other, but it was great that you did. We can't thank you enough for all you have done for us."

"Frank, it has truly been my pleasure. I have loved every

minute of time with you all and sincerely hope we will meet up again."

"Absolutely, honey, and it will be our turn to reciprocate. Can you give me your momma's address? I would like to drop her a line and just let her know what a wonderful son she has raised."

"Awe, thank you ma'am, um, Linda. That is so very kind of you. I will be sure to give it to Brooke and she can share with you." Bridger leaned in to give Linda a hug. "It has been so good to meet you and spend time with you."

"If you ever get back to the States, you have to come see us!" Linda dabbed at her eyes. She hated to be leaving such a wonderful young man. She knew there was no way he and Brooke could be together now, but he was such a perfect complement to her over-achieving self. He was confident and interesting, kind, and worldly. If only they were living on the same continent, at least. "We had better rest our weary bodies before another big day tomorrow. Brooke, we will see you, what, at about seven for breakfast?"

"That sounds perfect, Mom. You two rest well."

Brooke turned to Bridger. "Well, let's get that address out of the way before I forget. Shall we get some coffee?"

"Yes, thank you. I was afraid you would turn in for the night, too. I have to tell you, it's getting harder and harder to stay away from you."

They took a seat in the lounge and ordered coffee.

"You really outdid yourself with tonight's meal. We absolutely did not expect you to pick up the tab, too. How can I ever repay you for the whole experience? You can tell that Mom and Dad had a great time and they both really fancy you."

"I think they are terrific too. The three of you seem to have such an easy time together. I mean, you know each other so well and anticipate what the others need. Honestly, it reminds me a lot of my own family and has made me a bit nostalgic. As far as repaying me..." Bridger reached over and lightly brushed Brooke's cheek with his fingers. "In time, I believe you will find a way."

They shared a smile that lingered until the coffee arrived.

They talked into the early morning hours, sharing more stories about their families, college years and work lives. They promised to stay in touch, with no expectations about frequency. They both had busy lives and didn't expect that to change in the near future.

By two-thirty a.m. Bridger and Brooke were both exhausted. "I hate to do this, but my alarm will go off in just a couple hours. I should at least try to get some sleep."

"Yeah, I know. Bridger, there are no words. Just… thank you. Thank you for being so kind to me and my family; for bringing a freshness to my life in places I had closed off."

"I feel like the fortunate one here. I have a wonderful life, I really do, but these few days have made it great. I'm sad to see you leave but excited for you to continue your journey. Oh! I almost forgot! I wanted to tell you about an option for the next leg of your journey. After you tour Hamburg tomorrow afternoon, you can drive up to Franconian Switzerland. It's a popular tourist destination, but at this time of year you should have no trouble getting a reservation to spend the night and then go on to Berlin the following day."

"I read about that region. I was concerned we might run into some dangerously icy roads this time of year."

"Yeah, there are ski slopes and it can get cold up there. But you shouldn't have any trouble with the roads this time of year. There are several brew houses to visit and it's incredibly picturesque. It's a popular place for mountain bikers and hikers. You can bump into some really fun visitors there too."

"That seems to be your specialty, Mr. Goins."

Bridger laughed. "Yeah, I have a knack for meeting great, and sometimes colorful, people." He embraced Brooke with his smile. "I've kept you long enough. You have a big day ahead of you. I must say good night."

Bridger gave Brooke a hug and turned to leave.

"Not so fast there, soldier." Brooke grabbed Bridger's arm and stepped in front of him. She reached up and coaxed his face closer to hers. She pressed her lips to his, for a brief moment that would last a lifetime. She pulled back sheepishly. "Oh, I hope that was okay."

"Okay? That was fantastic! If I would have known we could do that, I would have tried harder in Amsterdam." He graced her lips with one last brush of his and walked slowly away into the dark.

11

____

Bridger's recommendations were spot on. Brooke and her parents explored Franconian Switzerland, a respite following the emotionally draining tour of Nuremberg and all the war-related artifacts there. They found an incredibly affordable hotel that was built in the 1750s. The exterior was a sunny yellow and the interior rooms were equally inviting, spacious, and each had a balcony with a view of the mountains.

From the hotel they walked around the mountain town and to the base of a local castle. They took some fun photos before the evening grew dark. The reviews for the hotel food and local beer were excellent, so they walked back and took a seat in the hotel restaurant. Once again, the food was plentiful and tasty. It was the beer that caught Frank's attention.

"You know me; I don't drink much but this beer is so fresh that I could get a little too used to having it every day. Just imagine the pounds I would pack on!" Frank patted his slight potbelly. He was a large man who did a lot of physical labor at home on the ranch. He's never had to worry about gaining weight.

"That Bridger, he really has an eye for places, doesn't he? This area is just what the doctor ordered for us. Next time we travel we could stay here a few days and I would be happy as a pig in mud." Fresh air and open spaces spoke to Frank's soul.

They did for Brooke too, but she rarely took time to enjoy nature.

"I'd like to think he has an eye for people, too. He adored the two of you."

"And us him. I can't wait to get some photos printed and send them to his mom with a little note. I would want someone to do that for me. I'm sorry we won't be seeing him again on this trip." Linda had already penned a note to Mrs. Goins. She was a traditionalist with notes, whether thank-you notes, thinking of you notes or get-well wishes.

"Some glorious memories already made on this trip. I'm so excited for the rest of the days. It seems to fly by so fast with all we are cramming into our days. You know, Dad, we could stay here longer, if you want to skip some other sites we planned to visit."

"Oh, no, honey! Don't be rearranging things now. You've done such a fine job so far. This place will just give me a reason to make another trip here, right Linda?"

"That's right. I never thought I would see it in you, Frank, but I think you have caught the travel bug." The couple laughed.

"That's a good bug to have, Dad. I already know I could come back here and explore. I feel like we are hitting the highlights, but it will take a lot more time to see everything. It seems like, compared to the States, the country isn't huge but it's so rich with history and you just can't take that all in over a short period of time."

"That's right. I would definitely be interested in coming back. Maybe, after Lana and Pablo get married and everyone settles in again, we can talk to the others about making a family trip out of it. It's just too good not to share. And Brooke, you've been just a love to do all the planning and make all the arrangements. Your father and I know how much work it was for you and can't thank you enough."

"It's been my pleasure. I'm just so happy to see you both so relaxed and enjoying yourselves. You have both worked so hard and so long on the ranch."

Frank raised his beer stein to toast their good fortune to be together enjoying life in such a beautiful part of the world.

THEY FILLED each day of their vacation with fun and frolic. They ate, explored, joined tours, explored castles and medieval ruins, and ate some more.

"I have never had so much beer in my life! Even as a young man I didn't drink this much beer, but I've enjoyed every swallow." Frank took a drink of his beer as they sat at the airport in Berlin awaiting their flights home. They would all fly into New York; however, Brooke's flight was a few hours later than her parents'.

"Oh, what time is it in Atlanta? I feel I should call Lana and see how her plans are coming. I've not picked up the phone this entire trip, but I think it's time now."

"It's the middle of the night there, Mom. I don't think you should call just yet. I'm sure she would have gotten ahold of one of us if there was a problem. I have seen no emails or texts come through from her."

What Brooke didn't mention was that two days ago she formally applied for a new position in her firm. Monica let her know Jeff's position was posted, and Brooke asked that she walk her application packet to human resources. Brooke felt confident that she was a strong contender for the job.

"It will be nice to be back in our time zone. I'll have a better chance of reaching her then. I can usually catch Lana between the gym and the office in the morning or on her way home in the evening, except she has a lot of evening meetings. Anyway, she has that fancy wedding planner. I'm sure everything will be perfect."

"It will be. Have you thought about what you're wearing to the wedding?"

"Before we left, Lana and I exchanged some ideas. She suggested I fly into Atlanta for a weekend and we could go shopping. Maybe you should come too. We could have a little bridal luncheon or something special. We didn't have an engagement party or anything."

"I think it's great if you go, Mom. I just know I will be swamped when I get back to the office."

Brooke sat with Linda and Frank at their gate until it was time for them to board the plane. Linda was a bit emotional. "Honey, once again, it was a fantastic trip. We just can't thank you enough for all you did. We will talk about this for years to come. As soon as your father and I go through the photos, we will put together an album and bring it to the wedding. Your sisters will be so jealous!"

Brooke hugged each tightly. "You two stay safe. Make sure you find the right gate in New York! I will be in the air when you get home and it will be late so let's talk tomorrow."

"Yes, yes, that sounds perfect. We love you." After one last round of hugs, they headed down the jetway.

BROOKE PULLED her carry-on filled with chocolates and souvenirs to a restaurant near her gate. She would not have the same level of amenities on the flight home as she did on the Concorde flight. It was only mid-morning in Munich, but she was hungry. Probably anxiety, she decided, as in her head she kept running through all the things waiting at work. With the end of the year just several weeks away, she had accounts to wind down and planning to do for the new year on rollover accounts.

As she finished ordering a weisswurst and beer, her phone rang.

"Hey Bridger! How are you?" They had kept in touch by text and phone during the trip.

"Missing you. How is it going? Are you at the airport?"

"Yeah. Just saw Mom and Dad off and now I'm having a farewell Weisswurst. Wish you were here to join me."

"I wish I was too. Having a pilsner with that sausage?"

"You know it. I want the full effect."

"That sounds right. I hope you have a quick flight and you savor this vacation. Don't let your head jump back into work before you get there. It will steal all that relaxation you enjoyed these past couple of weeks."

"Sound advice. Thank you. How about you, what are you doing today? It's Saturday, right?"

"Yes, a day off for me. I'm helping some friends move into an apartment and then I'm sure we will find dinner in their new neighborhood. Julia, my buddy's wife, is a foodie and we like to compare notes on the local restaurants. It should be fun."

"That sounds like a good time. My food is just arriving; I'm going to let you go. We'll talk again soon, okay?"

"Sounds great. You have a pleasant trip. Looking forward to the next update."

"Bye, Bridger." Brooke smiled as she ended the call; a feeling of warmth and love lay like a shawl over her shoulders. She felt love, but not in a 'got to have you, fill my world, complete me' sort of way. It was deep in her cells. A knowing that someone special had entered her life. Although she did not see a future life alongside Bridger, she had an inkling that anything was possible, with faith and an open mind.

12

"It was just the most wonderful early Christmas present! They used that new plastic wood material so it will never rot, but it looks like the old redwood deck when it was first built. I'm just so surprised they could do it in..."

"Mom! Wait! Let me get my eyes open. I think I missed the first half of what you said."

"Oh, I'm sorry honey. You know, this time change has me all messed up. Your father and I have been up for hours."

"Mom, the deck. What were you saying?"

"Well, we got home from the airport yesterday, I guess it was about six, just before dusk started falling, and when we drove up to the house... you know, we left our pickup in the long-term parking at the airport. Anyway, we couldn't figure out what was going on with the house, until we pulled up closer. There was this giant red bow across the railing on the deck. When we got out and started looking at it we saw all new decking. You remember, the old deck was looking a bit tired and your father just hasn't had time to get out there and fix it. I guess I must have said something to Lana. She and Pablo gave us an early Christmas present by having our deck redone while we were away."

"Are you kidding me? That was the big surprise she was doing for you?"

"What do you mean, honey?"

"Well, Lana told me, shortly after her engagement announcement, that she and Pablo planned a surprise for you while we were away. I thought maybe they were having flowers delivered when you returned from vacation. No, she had to go and do... oh never mind. It sounds wonderful, Mom. What a special treat for you to come home to."

"Well, it is a nice thing. But our trip! I still can't get over it. A memory that will last a lifetime! I hope you know how grateful your father and I are for all you did to make it happen."

"Yeah, I do. So, beyond the new deck, was everything in good shape when you got home?"

"It was just like I left it. Apparently Pablo knows someone with a large construction company and he had them come from Illinois out here to build this. They drove out, spent a couple days staying at a hotel in town, and did the work. It must have cost them a fortune. Of course if we would have had it done by someone, we would have used local builders, but you can't look a gift horse in the mouth now, can you."

"No Mom, that's right. It was a very nice thing they did for you. Just think of all the late night chats you and Dad will have out there in the summer."

"Funny you should mention that. There are two big new Amish rocking chairs on the deck. Cute as a button. I can see your father and I out there, waiting for our children to arrive, grandchildren spilling out of the backseat and running up the steps to sit in Granny and Pappy's laps. Am I getting carried away or what?"

"It is a lovely picture, Mom. One day, it will be true."

"From your lips to God's ears, my dear. Speaking of which, your dad printed off a couple pictures with Bridger in them and I have a little card in the mailbox for his mother. What a special guy he is! Don't you just wish he lived closer? You two seem like a perfect fit for one another."

"Oh Mom, if wishes were horses..."

"I know, I know, but God works in mysterious ways, right?

You can't close your eyes to the spark we saw. I haven't seen you like that... well, never."

"Like what, Mom?" Brooke truly did not know what her mother and father might have seen. She was not overtly flirtatious and there were no public displays of affection.

"So relaxed, confident, at ease in your own skin in the presence of a handsome, kind and capable man."

"I'll have to think on your observations. I'm happy I met him. We had a magnificent time together, and it was all such a strange coincidence I don't think it's all soaked in yet. For today, I've got to get back to some level of normalcy. Tomorrow will be a big day in the office and it's all I can do not to drag myself in there today to get a jump start on what I know will be a huge workload."

"Don't you dare do that! It's Sunday and the day that you planned in your schedule to re-acclimate, do laundry, wind down and just soak in all the wonderful sights, sounds, and tastes you experienced over the past sixteen days. Give yourself the day. I probably shouldn't have called so early. I forgot your plane was later than ours, and you maybe don't have the reverse jet lag problem we have. It's just that I'm used to talking to you every day and knew you would want to hear about our gift."

"Yes, Mom. To everything, yes. Did you talk to Lana already? Let her know how thrilled you are with your gift?"

"Yes, we called her right away when we got home. Pablo was seeing patients at the hospital, but we got to thank Lana."

"How was she doing? Everything lining up for the wedding?"

"She sounded a little distracted, but I guess that's to be expected these days with so much going on to get ready for the wedding. I will fly to Atlanta in just under two weeks. Do you want to come along?"

"Oh Mom, I will have to see how things are at work when I go in tomorrow. I'm not sure I will have time. But we do have a client there and it may be the right time to work in a business trip. I'll let you know."

"That would be super. I'm sure your sister would love to see you and talk through her plans."

"Yes, I'm sure she would too." *Lana loves an audience.* Brooke found it hard to let go of longstanding sibling rivalry between herself and the youngest daughter. It was so ingrained, and her reactions snuck up on her with no thought. Two years apart and the last to leave the nest, they vied for attention at home and school. Lana was always the prettiest, and was smart too. Brooke was the kind one, but kindness rarely attracts teenage boys.

Brooke wasn't jealous of the upcoming marriage of Lana and Pablo. Pablo was a pretty boy, the kind Brooke could not trust. She had a fleeting relationship in college with a popular pretty boy. Unfortunately, it wasn't just the two of them in the relationship. She learned the hard way that he was seeing other women behind her back despite their commitment to be exclusive. One bad experience was all it took for her to surround herself with obtrusive neon yellow caution tape.

"Well, I've got our laundry in and your dad is out working the cows. I've got to stock the fridge and get caught up on the mail. Keep me posted on your week. I hope work is under control when you get there tomorrow and you can ease into it."

"Thanks Mom. I'll be in touch soon, when I have a handle on my workload. Love you Mom!"

"Love you too Brooke!"

Brooke hung up and took a personal inventory. Still sitting in bed under the covers, she was bone tired from travel across time zones. It felt like she had been away from work for months, and a churning gnawed at her stomach with thoughts of returning in the morning.

She got up and made coffee. Her little house was in good shape. She needed to dust and vacuum, but otherwise it was perfect. She had bought her house shortly after moving to Miami. It was a classic bungalow in a historic part of town. The wrap-around porch and the mother-in-law detached casita were the selling points for Brooke. She rented the smaller house to a young couple in college and made substantial progress paying down the mortgage. Following her father's advice, she lived below her means.

The refrigerator was bare, as usual. She rarely took time to cook for herself. Brooke threw laundry in, showered, and rushed to the store. She picked up some readymade deli salads and meat, fresh fruit, flavored waters and wine.

By two in the afternoon, Brooke found herself completely without energy and ready for bed. She took a nap and woke at dinnertime in a sleep stupor. She forced herself to get out of bed and stay up for a while. Fleeting thoughts of sending a message to Bridger passed, as she was too tired to pen a meaningful message. Her mother and father left another message, once again thanking her for the wonderful trip and the opportunity to meet their new friend, Bridger.

13

———————

*B*rooke woke early and went into the office to check her emails and schedule. She was already guzzling caffeine, knowing she would be dog tired by the middle of the afternoon.

"Good morning, Monica!"

Somewhat sheepishly and without the usual enthusiasm, Monica stopped in Brooke's doorway before dropping her lunch off in the employee lounge. "Good morning, Brooke. Good to see you back."

"Hey, when you get settled, come back here. I have something for you." Brooke had arrived at work with an armload of gift bags for her team and Ginny, Jeff Cuddy's assistant. She had gotten a variety of gifts, hoping at least something in each bag would please the recipient. Her team was a jovial group, and loved gag gifts. Those were not easy to find, but the beautiful chocolates and canned white sausages should be a welcome substitute.

"Sure Brooke. Just let me put some things away here."

MONICA DIDN'T KNOW if she should rush to get back to Brooke's office, or drag her feet and avoid her the entire day. She expected to see Hal in Brooke's office soon. The day after Monica took

86

Brooke's late afternoon call that made her late for the school performance, Hal asked to speak with her. She was embarrassed that he had seen her crying, but was comforted by his words and his promise to talk with Brooke about firm expectations. Monica was concerned about what Brooke's response might be, as Brooke didn't like to be wrong. But more central to whom she was, she would never want to hurt anyone. Monica regretted her moment of tears and wished she had been more forceful with Brooke and put her off until the following day. Her application for the open position would still have been timely.

Monica was in Brooke's office when Hal's assistant summoned Brooke to meet with him. Monica quickly grabbed the gift bags for herself and her family, thanked Brooke and slinked back to her desk. She had a ten o'clock support staff meeting. Hopefully Brooke would not be back to her office before then. Monica did not want to see Brooke after what she believed would be a kind but strong message from Hal. Brooke was excited as she gathered up Ginny's gift bag to drop off on the way to Hal's office.

GINNY WASN'T at her desk when Brooke dropped off the goodie bag. Hal was waiting for her at the door to his office. "Come on in Brooke. Have a seat at the table there."

"Thank you. I can't tell you how great it is to be back." That was only partially true, but Brooke said what she believed he wanted to hear.

"I'm sorry to say I haven't called you in today to catch up on your trip, although I do hope you had a fabulous time. We can talk about it some other time. While you were away, I happened to encounter your assistant, Monica, after a particularly upsetting call with you."

Brooke felt a knot growing in her stomach. She was confused. She and Monica never had words. There was no confrontation, and they had limited contact while Brooke was on vacation. "I'm sorry, Hal, I don't know what you're referring to."

"There was an evening, it was about six and I saw Monica

leaving in tears. I followed up with her the next day, giving her time to handle whatever was bothering her. She informed me that you called while on vacation. She was just getting ready to leave for one of her children's school performances and you insisted she stay on the phone, making her miss the performance. I have to tell you she was quite upset, and frankly, so was I. I have worked hard to ensure that this firm puts family first. We value our employees too much to take them away from their family, especially for the important moments, like this was for Monica."

Brooke's heart dropped to her stomach. She would never have intentionally hurt Monica and had no recollection of insisting that Monica stay and do her work.

"Furthermore, I understand the work you asked Monica to do was related to your application for Jeff Cuddy's job. This incident shows me you don't currently possess, at the level I demand, the firm's philosophy, and I'll be the first to tell you that you are not an ideal candidate for the job. I will let the hiring committee do their work of vetting all the applicants, but if your name comes to me as their candidate I will have to think long and hard about promoting you to that position. I value you as an employee, Brooke. I'm just not convinced that you are ready for a promotion."

Tears stung Brooke's eyes. "I understand, sir. You have to know I would never have intentionally kept Monica from her daughter's performance. There clearly was a miscommunication. I take responsibility for that. I should not have been trying to do business while on vacation."

HER HEART SAT heavy in her chest. Her gut churned. She put on her professional mask, the one that showed only happiness and confidence, albeit false at the moment, and returned to her office. She closed the door and buried herself in work for the rest of the day. She reviewed the work the team did in her absence and sent kudos and corrections to them, taking extreme care to be positive and constructive.

Brooke wasn't sure how she would recover from this blow. It wasn't just the lost opportunity of the promotion, but the damage done to her relationship with Monica whom she respected a great deal. She was disappointed that Monica didn't say something to prepare her for the conversation with Hal. She felt blindsided.

Available to chat tonight? Dreadful day at work. Need to regroup. Her oldest sister, Robin, was the rock she turned to in moments like this where her emotions were too raw to make sense of things. Robin didn't hesitate to be there for her, and answered the text almost immediately. *I'm all yours, doll. Call whenever and I will be there for you.*

Brooke finished the workday and quietly left the building. Hopefully, tomorrow she would have the words and tools to navigate this rough water. She was discouraged, embarrassed, and jet lag overwhelmed her.

"I MEAN YOU KNOW ME, I would never insist that someone miss their child's school play. All I can figure is the connection was bad, and I didn't hear her say she needed to go. I think I need to talk to her, apologize, and find out what happened. How else am I going to know so I don't do it again?" She was recounting the events of the day for Robin while sipping wine in her cozy living room.

"Is the relationship with Monica one that you want to salvage?"

"Of course. She's a good person and does a good job. She's moody, but she also has a lot going on outside of work and it's stressful."

"Is the firm the place you want to continue to expend your energies and grow your career?"

"You know, right now that's something I'm no longer sure of. First, I have no family here in Miami. There is nothing about this community that makes my heart sing. I like my church, but it would be nice to have more in my life outside of work. Even my little house is just okay."

"And now for the pink elephant. How do you feel about not being considered for the promotion?"

"Initially I was sad, but the more I think about it I'm angry. I did not insist that Monica stay on the phone with me. If she needed to leave, and she knows this about me, I would never make her stay. For goodness sake, we are both grown women. She could leave whenever she needed to. She could have just hung the phone up and sent me a message. Seriously, our discussion was not a life or death one."

"I can understand that. Do you think Hal has a clear view of the circumstances?"

"I don't, but I'm not pressing to change his mind. He built the firm with his blood, sweat, and tears, with a dash of luck and a heaping serving of business savvy. But if I don't fit his vision of a valued employee that meets the firm's philosophy now, I never will. I don't feel a need to prove myself to him. I know at my core who I am and what I didn't do in this situation."

"That's my girl! You don't need to roll over and let them drag you down. You are talented. I've seen your work. You have the highest integrity and would never knowingly bring harm to anyone. As far as being away from family, I've said it before, and I'll say it again. Come on up here with me! I don't live in The Big Apple but I'm close enough to partake of the culture when I want. My company isn't hiring right now, but there are so many creative opportunities here I'm sure you wouldn't have any problem finding a job. I have a spare room you can use for as long as you want. I think it would be a lot of fun, a little reminiscent of having a bestie in college."

"Yeah, that could be a blast. I just don't know. I think I need a couple days to just sit with it and feel my feelings about it. I am not excited to be going back to work tomorrow, but you know me, I'll take the high road and do my job to the best of my abilities. I don't need these people to be my dearest friends, just to cooperate at the office. I will also stop giving up my free time. I don't get paid for working overtime since I'm salaried. That spirals me right back into asking myself what I would do with that free time with no family here. Aargh! This is not where I thought I would be on my first day back after a fabulous vacation."

"I heard from Mom yesterday. She was floating on cloud nine talking about the trip and some guy you all met there, Barry or something."

"Bridger."

"What?"

"His name is Bridger."

"No wonder I couldn't remember his name. I don't think I've heard that name before."

"It was new to me as well. It was a surname in a prior generation on his mother's side and she always loved the name."

"Anyway, he sounds like an impressive guy. Mom says she wished he was in the States. She thinks you two would be great together."

"Ha! That's Mom, the matchmaker. Actually, for me, meeting and spending time with Bridger was the highlight of the entire trip but everything about the trip was wonderful. Mom and Dad were so appreciative and there wasn't wedding talk every day, just half the days."

"That's a miracle in itself. Mom is such an obsessive planner. Sounds like she was on her best behavior."

"Speaking of Lana, did you hear…"

"Oh, yeah. Got the whole moment-by-moment reveal from Mom on the phone. All I can do is sigh. I know it's an ego boost for Lana, but it saddens me that she needs an ego boost. She's such a beautiful, capable woman, but for whatever reason, she is monumentally insecure. It's her burden and I can't own it or try to protect her. I used to try, but then I looked at her life, which seemed really peachy to me, and I let it go. We all have the same parents. It's hard to fathom why she is the way she is."

"Yeah, it took me some time to sort it out. Being the next in line to her I probably couldn't see the forest for the trees until I was away from home for a couple of years. And by then I was so immersed in my own world I couldn't track hers. Mom, however, still treats her like a high schooler. If I'm totally honest with myself, I still have twinges of jealousy. I notice it more with all the wedding talk."

"Back to you, my dear. Let's stay in touch, and if you need some moral support tomorrow I am just a call away. We are editing our latest project now so I can break away almost anytime."

"You are my angel on earth, Robin. I hope you know how much you mean to me."

"I do know you appreciate me as I do you. We have to stick together."

"Through thick and thin. I'm sure I'll be in touch tomorrow."

"Perfect. Try to be at ease tonight and know that you can choose something far greater, if you want. You may not know what that is right now, but as they say if one door closes then a better one opens."

"Thanks for that. I will write it down now and remind myself. Keep me in your prayers."

"Always. Bye."

14

———

*B*rooke struggled to enjoy work and co-workers in the office throughout her first week back. She was cordial, pleasant even, but didn't go out of her way to make brownie points like she previously did.

In the evening, she soaked in inspiration and acceptance from Robin, exchanged messages with Bridger, and checked in with her mom and dad. Linda talked more and more about Lana's upcoming nuptials - who was wearing what, the venue, the reception food, and Pablo. Brooke half listened until her mother turned the conversation to Bridger.

"Have you talked to Bridger, honey? His mother should have her card about now. I hope she enjoys the photos."

"Bridger and I chat online, Mom. He's working on plans to entertain his mom when she comes at Christmastime. He's run several ideas by me. I think they will have a fantastic time, even though he has to work most of the time and they won't get to travel extensively like we did."

"Oh, I'm sure he will make it special. I got to show some pictures to my ladies' group. They loved seeing them and hearing about all the places we went. There were some shots of you and Bridger. Everyone was excited to see you with a man in the pictures."

"Oh Mother! Really? I told you, we are too far away from one another to be serious. He's just a new friend I had the wonderful fortune of meeting while on vacation." Brooke had not, and did not plan to, tell her mother or father about the tongue-lashing she received on returning to work. She didn't want to burden them with blow-by-blow stories of her misadventures at work or her soul-searching to determine what her next steps would be, if any.

On the second day back to work, Brooke had a subdued conversation with Monica about their misunderstanding. She apologized for causing Monica to miss her daughter's event. Monica thanked her but took no responsibility for any part of the situation. That was all it took for Brooke to emotionally distance herself. She took this as a sign to herself that all was not well for her in the current environment.

Always intuitive, Brooke experienced a sense of *knowing* when she needed to make a change. In college, before entering junior year, she had a strong pull to change schools. She was drawn to a small college that gave her opportunities to lead and explore new levels of personal growth. By making this single move, her resume evolved three-fold.

Before she bought her home, Brooke made an offer on another property. Upon finding her current home, with the added opportunity for rental income, she rescinded the offer on the first property and purchased her home. She later learned that the other house had hidden issues that would have continually drained her bank account, without the benefit of rental income.

Intuition influenced all her life. Now, it was telling her to move on. Unfortunately, there were no specifics as to where she should go or what she should do.

Her heart pulled her toward time with Robin, but from a career and homeowner perspective she wasn't sure what to do. She examined the tenderness related to the ego hit of being reprimanded and presumed guilty without an adequate investigation. It was no accident that this moment came. She looked deeper for meaning.

"I mean, I just don't know what all this means. My heart and my gut are telling me this job has been my playground. A place to explore and learn and grow. I've made a good run of it. Not everyone my age has the opportunity to manage multi-million dollar accounts, unfettered travel to bond with clients and grow a relationship, and manage a team of creatives. I am grateful for all those opportunities. There is something missing for me though."

"What would that be?" Robin never tired of exploring life with her sister. She was attentive and encouraging at every turn. That's what Brooke would be for her and she had been, but more as a sounding board for her personal relationships. Robin loved being alone and spending time with friends; she was not drawn toward romantic relationships. She accepted that part of herself long ago, but tired of defending her singleness within the family. Friends accepted her as she was. They became her family of choice. Brooke understood that.

"I think it's a life with more color, more joy and more travel," Brooke answered, feeling free to speak truthfully with this sister. "The trip to Europe opened my eyes to all the possibilities for travel. It's safe, reasonably affordable, and was easy even with Mom and Dad. I'm wondering if there is a way to pair my journalism minor, my marketing major, travel and enjoying a decent life."

"Oh, girl, you are giving me goosebumps! I don't know what that is, but I believe for you it's possible. Look at all the travel magazines and travel agencies. They get their articles and photos from somewhere. I'm sure they use freelancers to feed the industry."

"That makes sense. Do you think it seems like something I should investigate?"

"I do. I have some author friends. Let me check with them for any insights they might have. I think it sounds like a cool lifestyle. I know you like your home and have made it really cozy there. How do you feel about being on the road and not having a home to go to overnight or even a home base that you call your own, at least for a while?"

"I'm actually getting excited about the possibility of more

travel. I never before allowed myself to dream of doing anything
but going into an office and doing the grind. Thanks so much for
the inspiration."

BROOKE DIDN'T RUSH into submitting her resignation. For two
weeks she investigated freelance jobs that would give her the
freedom to travel that she wanted. It was something she had
thought about while in college, but hadn't dared to indulge in
because she couldn't see a way to be the responsible contributing
member of society she was raised to be.

She also took time to write goal lists, study pros and cons of
potential courses of action and allowed herself to dream. She
pulled her leather-bound journal out of the nightstand drawer.
For three years in a row she had started this journal in January
with promises to write daily, to be faithful to herself in docu-
menting her thoughts and give space for her feelings, only to tuck
it back in the drawer a few days later.

At the suggestion of the one friend outside her family who she
confided in, she drafted a list of attributes she would like in a
partner. She knew she wanted one. She started the list: kind,
generous, witty, likes to travel, high level of integrity, excellent
communicator, respectful, trustworthy.

Bridger was the only man she was in semi-regular contact
with. She tried not to pepper him with questions the way a
researcher would, but some topics came up in their conversations.
She asked questions about how he handled conflict, his thoughts
on debt, and how he balanced his personal time and social time.
She already knew he had a great relationship with his mother and
met all of the first ten things she put on her list.

As she explored the list, she reflected on happy couples she
knew, couples that had been together for many years. What attributes did they each bring to the table? She listed the qualities she
saw in each of those individuals and then compared herself to the
list. She quickly realized that her life experiences were quite

limited in the realm of relationships. Like her sister Robin, she quite enjoyed being alone. Perhaps she wasn't relationship material after all.

She thought about her sister Julie's marriage to Keith. She called Julie one Saturday afternoon just to chat.

"I want to interview you." Brooke saw this as an opportunity to practice her journalism skills.

"Interview me? Really? I'm not all that interesting."

"Consider it a favor to me. I'm thinking of writing a series of articles. My working title is *Relationships on the Road*. In doing my background work, I realized that I really know little about long-term relationships and what makes them work."

"Well, I guess we just celebrated our ten-year anniversary. That probably counts as long-term. Fire away."

Brooke walked through the list of questions she had prepared. She gathered some background information about the couple like how they met, their dating life and the decision to marry. She already knew the answers, she thought, but wanted to practice the questions for other interviews.

As she continued with the more probing questions about their relationship, Julie shared some unexpected things. Brooke learned that like Lana, Julie struggled with deep-seated self-esteem issues. In the first half of their marriage she was perpetually suspicious of Keith having an affair, with no justification whatsoever. It created a great deal of stress in their relationship and led to distancing and unhappiness.

Julie revealed that now, with hindsight and some therapy, she realized she married too young to feel loved, and out of fear that nobody else would find her desirable. She was tearful yet open as she shared. "Don't get me wrong. I love Keith. I just sometimes wonder if I would have a different lifestyle had I believed more in myself and my ability to attract an accomplished partner. It may change nothing, but maybe I wouldn't have to work and could dedicate my time to the important work of charities."

. . .

After the interview, Brooke drew in a deep sigh. She sat on the porch with a cup of hot tea and reviewed her notes. She wondered if anyone was truly happy; if everyone walked around wearing a plastic mask of happiness.

The more she pondered this question, not only for herself but also on a larger scale, the more disheartened she became. She grew suspicious of the tenents she learned growing up. Get a good job. Work hard. Settle down. Raise a family. Put your time in. Retire and enjoy life.

Why did the enjoyment come at the end instead of getting infused throughout? Did the rest really have to be drudgery that lasted for years, in the hopes that you would live to retirement? Brooke wanted to flip that paradigm for herself. She wanted joy each step of the way; she just needed to work out what that looked like. There was one thing she knew for certain - staying in her job for the sake of having a good job and being a rising young professional was not joy. She was capable of so much more.

15

———

y December first, Brooke knew that she would start the coming new year out fresh. She met with a realtor and listed her house. Her tenants were sorry to see her go and would love to purchase the home, but they were not financially able to while still in school. Brooke assured them that the sale would include lease terms to protect the renters. They were good people and perfect tenants. She wanted them to have the option to stay, without a change in their reasonable rent. Her seemingly impulsive decision to uproot herself should not negatively impact them. Brooke made a mental note to donate her pantry items and remaining liquor to this young couple when she did leave. They weren't big drinkers, but when their budget allowed, they enjoyed an occasional celebratory beverage.

Brooke had three offers in the first two days the house was on the market. A bidding war followed, and she accepted an offer that was five percent over the asking price. The buyers also bought the furnishings, none of which were family heirlooms or irreplaceable. They were anxious and ready to move in as soon as possible, and Brooke was now more than ready to move on. The closing date was December 30, just three weeks away.

Only personal effects would go with her to New York. She

took Robin up on the offer to use her spare room as a home base. Things just seemed to fall into place. Brooke's dream, to travel and write, was becoming reality.

Brooke became so involved in her own activities that she gave little thought to Lana, Pablo, and their wedding, other than to secure an airplane ticket and contribute to the sibling-group gift. Julie collected a hundred dollars from each of them and would choose a suitable gift from the group. Lana prearranged the hotel room for all of the family. There was little to do for the occasion.

In mid-December she gave her notice at the office. With accumulated leave and holidays, that left only two short workweeks for her last days there.

Shortly after receiving her letter of resignation, Bob, her direct supervisor, stopped by her office. "Brooke, I feel just awful about how this all went down. I should have intervened. I need you to know I think the firm is losing a brilliant talent. You have done exceptional work. Whatever happened between you and Monica was clearly a misunderstanding, but since Hal intervened my hands were tied. I do think you were the top runner for Jeff's replacement. You have shown an exceptional ability to engage with and inspire our clients. They are sad to see you go too. I've received several calls asking if there was some way we could talk you into staying."

"Thanks for those kind words, Bob. That whole crazy thing with Hal really gave me the pause I needed to do some self-evaluation and chart a new course for my life."

"Do you know what's next for you? You can count on me for a glowing reference."

"I will be working, initially at least, as a freelance writer. I've already submitted a few articles to test the waters and they have been well received. My house sold within hours so I have that money to fall back on. My living expenses will be low. I think I'll have a year or two of exploring and building a new career that gives me the freedom to travel and explore the world the way I want to. I appreciate being able to rely on you for a reference. In fact, I don't think it would hurt if I had a letter in my back pocket. Would you mind putting that together for me?"

"Absolutely. I'll have it for you tomorrow. Your team has asked to throw a farewell for you. I wanted to check with you to see if that's something you want."

"Well, I hadn't thought about it. Honestly, I would prefer to do something away from work. Maybe we can just go out after work one night as a small group."

"I understand. I'll let them know." Bob reached out and took Brooke's hand and held it in his. "Let's not be strangers. I am so happy for you to be embarking on this adventure. I wish you all the best."

"Thank you, Bob. I'm very excited to see what will come. I'll look for that reference tomorrow."

Brooke's team was sorry to see her go and Monica was distant. Hal was on his annual vacation so she was able to avoid any more dealings with him. She even skipped the holiday party. Brooke left for Christmas vacation and never returned.

BROOKE WAS OPTIMISTIC, confident and excited to be on this new adventure. "Robin, I can't thank you enough for all you have done for me. Without you as a cheerleader, I'm not sure I would be following my passion right now. I don't think I can ever repay you."

"You wait till you get here, hun. I'm sure I'll find a way for you to make it up to me. I might need a few late night chats of my own."

"I'll be there for you. You can count on that. And thanks for that lead on the Bo-Ho Travel Magazine, too. I had a great exchange with their hiring manager, submitted two articles from my trip to Germany and they loved them. In fact, I'll be meeting with them in early January about some regular work. They loved my article about the castle wedding."

"I'm so happy for you! You'll be traveling the world in no time."

The sisters' daily chats inspired them both. Robin was happy to freshen up her apartment and clear old boxes out of the spare bedroom for Brooke to move in. It was an added bonus to hear about Brooke's changes that she didn't even know she had inspired.

Brooke read all the articles she could find online about transitioning from corporate life to freelancing. She reached out to a few authors through the emails associated with their bylines. Two of them agreed to talk with her about their experiences. From this, she gained valuable information about the realities of working as a freelancer. Financially, she was prepared to support herself for an extended period. She grew confident in her ability to find work and had some early networking under her belt.

The one area she wasn't comfortable with was working alone all the time. There was something about interpersonal relationships that was critical to living a purposeful life. She loved exchanging ideas with others and found that boosted her creativity. She joined online communities of writers and artists, but knew she would need a physical outlet as well. She was now journaling daily and kept a running to-do list, always including a reminder to prioritize searching for meaningful face-to-face volunteer opportunities after she moved.

As she sorted and packed, Brooke developed an initial plan. When she left for Lana and Pablo's wedding, she would leave behind her old life and start anew with a refreshed outlook. The most difficult farewells were those at church. The choir, in particular, was a group of people she enjoyed being with. They were excited to follow Brooke on her journey, and all promised to keep in touch.

Linda and Frank were not entirely surprised by Brooke's decision, although perplexed and worried by the rush of it all. They were supportive of her following her dreams and offered their home, should she ever find herself in need or just wanted to spend time with them. It was a relief to Brooke when they verbalized their support. Her feeling of obligation, to fit what she thought was their mold for her, started to dissolve.

Her parents often talked about Bridger. Linda spoke to his mother on the phone after they first exchanged notes. Immediately after that conversation, she called Brooke. "Bridger's mom, Margie, has such a beautiful spirit. Bridger talks about you all the time, keeping her updated on your life changes. She wishes only the best for you. She leaves for Germany on Wednesday. She is so excited to be spending Christmas with him."

"I hope they get some free time to travel," Linda continued excitedly. "We saw such wonderful places while we were there and I know Bridger would like to show her around. It all depends on his work and whether any assignment comes up for him that can't be delayed until after the holiday. She understands that. She's so proud of her boy and his service. She also loves that he has adventures and shares them with her. He's a good son."

Brooke noted yet another attribute from her life partner list in Bridger's favor. He was close to his mother, and that was enough for Brooke to know what kind of person he was. Despite all the wonderful things about Bridger, she knew this wasn't the time to abandon her dreams and chase a man. She needed to, and wanted to, join whatever relationship she ultimately chose as a whole person, with dreams and aspirations, hidden talents unveiled and insecurities moved out of the way. It wouldn't be easy to be that person but she firmly believed she was on the way to becoming the woman she envisioned, at least on the next step of her life's grand adventure.

BROOKE LEFT Miami on December 30 with two sizable pieces of checked luggage and carried onboard a laptop and a small bag with her best jewelry and a few personal items. The postal service would deliver the rest of her belongings, in eleven boxes, to

Robin's apartment. Once the decision to move was made, she found it easy to pare down belongings and lighten her footprint. She donated all her business suits except for one, just in case she needed it for a face-to-face interview. The dress shop had sent her dress for the wedding directly to the hotel. She kept only one pair of dress shoes, which were tucked securely in her carry-on.

16

———

ana and Pablo's wedding was a joyous family reunion. Every detail of the event was stylized and dazzling, just like the matrimonial couple. Pablo's mother was an absolute delight. Vanessa was a beautiful, petite woman with deeply caring blue eyes and blonde hair. She was a tenured professor at a college in a Chicago suburb and taught graduate level philosophy.

At the rehearsal dinner, the night before the nuptials, the group gathered at a local Italian restaurant. Linda was alarmed to see close familiarity between Pablo and a young woman who unexpectedly showed up. Marriage alone would not dissolve her protective shield of Lana. Pablo would have to earn her trust. Linda leaned across the table to Brooke and Robin. "Who is that? Look at her hugging Pablo!"

"Maybe it's his cousin, or a childhood friend." Robin guessed.

Vanessa seemed equally happy to see the young woman, and then Lana hopped up from the table and joined the three. Linda was relieved to realize that the attractive young woman was Pablo's sister, Annabelle, making a surprise appearance. The army had granted a brief leave from her post in Afghanistan.

Lana held her hand out. "Oh my, Annabelle, it's so wonderful to meet you!"

Annabelle threw her arms around Lana and squeezed hard. Lana was red-faced when the embrace ended. "My sister! I can't believe I have a sister! I've always wanted one. My goodness, you are more beautiful than I imagined. You look absolutely radiant. I hope it's okay that I am crashing your party."

"Oh, my goodness! You aren't crashing anything. It's so wonderful you could join us." Lana looked up to Pablo, who radiated joy that his baby sister could join them. "Can I steal your sister? I have a few of my own I would like her to meet."

"Mind if I tag along?" Pablo escorted the women to Lana's family table.

"If I may have your attention, please," he announced proudly. "We have a very special guest with us this evening. I am delighted to introduce to you Private First Class Annabelle Porta."

"Pablo, your sister! Annabelle, I'm so pleased to meet you. I'm Linda, Lana's mother."

"Yes, this is my baby sister. She surprised us by showing up just now. I had no idea she would join us." Pablo put his arm around his sister's shoulders and Lana's waist. "It fills my heart with great joy to have our families here. This is really a special time."

He nodded to his mother, and they shared a smile.

"Let me have them set a place for you, Annabelle. We're just ordering our first round of drinks. You arrived at the perfect time."

"Thank you, Lana. I'm thrilled to be here."

"Come, sit down, tell us about your trip. It must have taken you quite awhile to get here." Frank was happy for the wedding couple to have this special surprise.

"Yes, sir, it has been many hours, what with the clearance and all, but it's worth every boring moment sitting on that plane and in those barracks. This is the event of the century for my family. Pablo's been so dedicated to his education and his work that we weren't sure he would ever have time to find a wife. And such a lovely one at that!"

"Aren't you the sweetest? It's hard to believe we have soldiers as beautiful as you over there, protecting our country." Linda was taken by the beautiful, petite young woman with coarse dark hair, almond eyes and coppery skin.

"Thank you. I'm just one of many women serving. It's my honor."

"As you can imagine, her family is really proud of her. She's destined for fantastic things, this girl of mine." Vanessa slid next to Annabelle and put her arm around her waist. "It's so lovely to see her out of uniform and in a dress. I haven't seen those legs for a while."

Vanessa turned to the table. "We get to video chat, but she's always in uniform and I get the head and shoulders view. A mother needs to see their whole child occasionally to feel assured."

"Well I, for one, am so grateful you're here. Pablo, honey, it looks like everyone has their drink. Could you get a glass for Annabelle? I think a toast is in order."

Pablo leaned in and kissed his bride-to-be. "You are absolutely right, honey."

He looked to Annabelle. "Can you handle a glass of champagne?"

"I think I can. Can you?" The two chuckled at what seemed to be an inside joke between the siblings.

Robin leaned into Brooke and whispered. "She seems like a sweet kid. I'm still not sure about him though."

Brooke snuck in a thumbs-up below the table's edge and continued to smile with the other guests.

"So Brooke, tell us about your upcoming adventure. Where do you think you'll go first?" Julie wanted to be excited for Brooke, but her conservative, traditionalist outlook gave her pause. She hoped this new lifestyle worked for her sister, since she really had no ties with children and now no house either.

"It looks like I have an opportunity to get to some resorts in Thailand in February. I also have an interview with a company that would like me to write a series of stories like the one I wrote about a castle wedding in Germany. Robin introduced me to someone a friend of hers knows. It was a great opportunity to get my foot in the door and I brought a fresh idea to them that they want to jump right on for the new year. Actually, the more I think about this, I think I will have an opportunity to do some market consultation, too."

"That sounds fascinating."

"It's still a leap of faith for me. I pray every day for guidance and Mom, I have you to thank for inspiration. Do you remember that day at Heidelberg Castle when you designed that whole wedding reception in the courtyard?"

"Oh, honey, I remember that day and I could see it so vividly in my mind's eye - the flowers, candelabras and crystal. You did a fantastic job writing that article. You captured it perfectly."

"I should probably give you a finder's fee, Mom."

"I'm looking forward to living vicariously through you as you travel the world. Maybe we can even meet up somewhere."

"That would be fun, wouldn't it? Let's see, it's a few years until your fortieth anniversary, but if we start planning now maybe we could all do something exotic together." Julie, like her mother, had a little of the party planner in her. "Keith and I have talked about traveling when the kids get a little older. We enjoyed the one out-of-country we took, didn't we hun?"

"We sure did. We took a cruise down through Cabo and enjoyed the total freedom it gave us. No kids, no cooking, no decisions to make except what we wanted to eat and what we wanted to wear. It was wonderful." Keith looked lovingly at his wife, then to their young daughters. "Maybe it will even be a trip you girls can join us for."

Savannah and Tilly were excited to be involved in the grown-up events. Savannah, the nine-year-old, was petite, reserved, fair and sweet. She was the spitting image of her mother. "That would be very nice, Daddy."

"Daddy, I think we should go to Costa Rica. They have the coolest animals there. I even saw a giant snake hanging from a tree on TV." Tilly was the family clown and athlete. She was a promising young gymnast, feared nothing, and loved the animal shows on television. "Auntie Brooke, do you think we could go with you to Costa Rica someday?"

"I would like nothing more, Tilly. I will keep you posted. Look, Auntie Lana has something to say." Brooke raised her finger to her lips, letting the girls know it was time to be quiet and pay attention to Lana and Pablo.

"Attention, please. Attention." Pablo and Lana stood together at the head of the table. A picture-perfect couple. "Friends and family, Lana and I want to thank you for being here with us tonight. Even you Danny." Pablo raised a finger and pointed it at his best man, Dan. The two were fraternity brothers. Dan, once a college football player, was now an orthopedic surgeon in Arizona. "We will forgive you forgetting the rings for rehearsal, but you better have them tomorrow!"

"No problem man, I know right where they're at… I think." The group laughed.

"Annabelle, would you come here and join us, please? We have a very special guest with us this evening. U.S. Army Private First Class, Annabelle Porta. My sister somehow managed to get leave from her station in Afghanistan to join us. Lana and I, and Mom of course, are so thrilled to have you here with us. If you would, please, raise your glass and toast my beautiful sister and our soldier, Annabelle."

The group, which filled the private room in a swanky restaurant, erupted in clinks and cheers for Annabelle. Pablo continued to introduce all the guests and Lana said a few words before they ate. Between dinner and dessert, Vanessa said a few words, gushing over her handsome, accomplished son and wishing the couple well. She passed the floor to Frank who humbly spoke of his love for his family, the joy Lana brought as the baby of the family, and the strong family values held by the Linton family.

Frank finished with a toast. "To all of you, from all of us - my wife and myself, Lana, and our entire family. Pablo, welcome to the family and thanks for making Lana's dreams come true. Thank you for bringing this group of wonderful people together. If it weren't for you, we would not be making glorious memories together. Annabelle, thank you for your efforts to be here in celebration, and thank you for your service. Let's raise our glass to the soon-to-be Mr. and Mrs. Porta. Here's to a memorable wedding and a lasting marriage filled with love!"

AFTER THE PARTY, Lana joined the family in the executive suite she had reserved for her family. The four sisters talked until the wee hours of the morning. They looked at photos from the trip to Germany. Robin shared a mini film she was working on depicting violence against women across the world. The film was her contribution to a fundraising effort on behalf of the mentally ill and homeless in New York City. Julie shared stories about the girls and a video of a dance recital they were in.

Lana shared… Lana. She talked about how she and Pablo were handling their two condos, bringing their tastes together into one new place they were purchasing. "My place had a buyer within hours of going on the market and his within two days. The market is just really hot right now."

"So Brooke, tell us about this mystery man you met in Germany." Julie pointed to a picture of Bridger in a photo album Frank and Linda brought.

"There's no mystery, really." Brooke shared their funny chance meeting in Amsterdam. "And when he said I was looking in the wrong country, with that crooked grin on his face, I knew he was witty and playful. It was just the way he said it."

"Did you really sing karaoke? Did he sing with you?" Julie had sent Keith and the girls to bed long before and she kept drinking champagne. She was the most relaxed Brooke had seen her in years.

"I did. It was a blast!"

"Did you have to sing in German? Did he sing, too?"

"No, and emphatically no. I don't speak German but they listen to a lot of American music. As far as Bridger singing, he said his church kicked him out of the choir and that he is tone deaf. I didn't push the issue. It's probably true, but he had a blast anyway. He seemed to like my voice."

"Oh, I bet he did, and the package that comes with it." Robin wanted in on this conversation.

"Guys, he is the most respectful man I've ever met. It's just too bad he is married to the military. I would pursue him if he were closer to home."

"We'll see. Your home is becoming mobile and I doubt you would have to pursue him. He would be hot on your trail."

"That's what he says. I'm happy for him that he gets to travel and see the world. One day, he will be the one to be closer to his mom to help her as she ages."

"Ah, what a wonderful guy. Pablo is like that, too. He is so close to his mom and sister that I feel like a third wheel. I guess that would be fourth, when they are together. Even on video chats."

"Just wait until you have a family. That will change. It did for Keith. He was a real momma's boy until he had a child of his own." The transformation Keith made when Savannah was born astounded Julie. He suddenly became a warrior and protector of his family. It was a fascinating study in human evolution.

"We shall see. Right now, he's at the hospital or clinic all the time, even on weekends. I have to make a date with him to spend any time, it seems." A sadness filled Lana's eyes. To avoid bringing the party down, she glanced up, grabbed the bottle of champagne and added some to each sister's glass. "And now, my opportunity to toast all of you! I know I'm the baby and have been a pain for you over the years, but tomorrow I will become Pablo's better half. I raise my glass to you, my sisters! Each of you has helped me get to this point in my life and I am grateful God put us in the same family. You are blessings and angels to me."

"Cheers!" The women spoke loudly, and in unison.

Julie giggled and spoke in a whisper. "Oh no! I hope we don't wake the others up. We're out of bubbly and have nothing to share with them."

In silence the sisters sat and finished their drinks, lost in thought to days gone by, the big day tomorrow, and dreams of the future new year.

As expected, the wedding was beautiful. The reception was fun, and everyone was on his or her best behavior. Lana sparkled with joy; her groom was attentive and appeared happy. Maybe they were wrong about him. Time passed quickly. The big wedding day was over and the New Year had begun.

17

"I hope, for Lana's sake, Pablo lives up to his appearances. I really do want her to be happy." Robin and Brooke were in a cab on the way to the airport.

"That's one thing I would be happy to be wrong about, and did you notice, she wasn't the little princess she used to be? She was genuinely kind and considerate to all of her guests. Marriage may look good on her." The maturing of their baby sister impressed Robin. It seemed as if Lana had arrived at the next phase of her life and left behind some childishly selfish ways. Now, the rest of the family needed to acknowledge and reinforce that maturity.

"Can I just say, I'm happy that's behind me?" Brooke bit her bottom lip. "That sounds more mean than I intend it to, but I'm so ready to get started on my fresh life. You know, we never did decide on what my rent will be."

"Actually, we did. I told you I would not accept any rent. I'll tell you what you can do for me though. You can cook sometimes when you're home." Robin patted her stomach. "I eat out way too much and it shows. I wouldn't mind some grilled salmon and fresh salad once in a while and maybe we can even throw a little dinner party once in awhile? I choose not to cook. It takes too much time and I have so many leftovers that just go to waste."

"Oh, I know what you mean. That's one thing about the holidays I love. I enjoy cooking and entertaining. But unless there is some big celebration going on, I don't do it. I think the way we were raised, not poor but certainly not rich, we learned to use every last scrap of food we had. It's hard for me to throw things away, but honestly, there's only so many leftover casseroles you can stuff in a refrigerator freezer. When I moved I had several perfectly good meals that I gave to my tenants. They were thrilled and I was happy not to waste the food."

"You will be around until later in January at least, right?"

"It looks like it. I have several more leads to follow up on and more articles to write for my portfolio."

"Do you think you would be up to a little shindig at our place in a couple of weeks? I have talked so much about you to my friends and some coworkers. I think they would love the opportunity to come over and meet you."

"Well, sure. Are you thinking about dinner or just heavy appetizers?"

"Oh, gosh. Heavy appetizers sounds like a lot of fun. Isn't it a lot of work though?"

"Nah, it doesn't have to be. I have an entire file of recipes I've saved for the day I could throw a party. I'll pick a few recipes and grab two or three pre-made things at the deli to add to the mix. I'm happy to get wine and beer too. Do you think anyone will want cocktails? We could do one special mix for the evening or just open the bar."

"About that. I don't have much of a bar at home, but I do know a couple of favorite drinks. I'll get the spirits and mixers. I probably need a few more glasses, too. You'll hear from my friends that I've turned into a workaholic hermit over the past few years. I need you as much as you need me right now. Maybe I'll even get a stylish haircut and up my wardrobe game."

"Well, if you want. You're beautiful, and of course I think you're a genius, so if you want to add the sparkly things that require more upkeep, that's on you."

"Oh, excellent point! I've been pretty happy having hair I can just pull back to keep out of my face while I'm working."

"That's the direction I'm headed. I don't want to be traveling the globe with one suitcase dedicated to makeup and hairstyling gadgets. If it doesn't fit in my backpack, I don't need it."

"Atta girl! Say, it was fun watching you talk about Bridger last night. Do you know you light up like a little schoolgirl with her first crush when you talk about him?"

Brooke swatted at the air between her and Robin. "Oh, stop. That's not true."

"Okay, if you say so."

As if on cue, Brooke's phone chimed. *Thanks for sending the wedding photo. Beautiful couple and family. Glad you made it through and can carry on with your own dreams now. Keep it light. B.* Bridger understood her. He recognized her work-harder tendencies. She was grateful for his gentle reminder.

Robin saw the smile cross her beautiful sister's face as she read the message. Brooke wasn't ready for more with Bridger. She needed to enjoy her developing new world and establish her independent success first, using her abundant creativity and competence. For now, she was content with the way things were.

Robin recognized the cocoon emerging Brooke was preparing to do. Robin had come out of her protective incubator once, too. She had a mentor to guide her - a female film-school professor who was an extraordinarily gifted film artist and teacher. Professor Martin encouraged Robin to explore arts films and several film projects. She introduced Robin to a wide variety of individuals in the industry and helped build her confidence.

Unfortunately, as Robin grew closer to graduation and independence, Professor Martin showed her true colors. She became possessive and manipulative and expressed an unwelcome romantic interest. Robin was confused. She questioned everything she believed about herself. But she was graduating, and had to decide either to go out into the wide world and put to use all the great education she received, or retreat to the familiar life she knew in Kansas. She chose to fly and never regretted the decision.

In the early years after graduating, Robin worked a second job in a coffee shop in the arts district, hoping to make connections and keep a steady but small income flowing. Now, she had a great reputation and a modest following in the industry and was an up-and-coming filmmaker in her own right. She saw the same opportunity for Brooke to become an independent artist in her own right, without the drama she had endured.

Two short weeks later, Brooke met some of the friends Robin made during those early days in New York. There were two co-workers from the coffee shop that absolutely adored Robin. James and Alana both moved on with their careers since they all worked together. Alana worked as a middle school teacher and James, an interesting philosophy and visual arts major, had published his first book while working as an editor for a large publishing company. It was a fun reunion for the three of them.

A very pregnant Marcia and her husband Jon stopped by for an hour. Marcia was Robin's first roommate in the city. Robin answered an ad for a roommate posted at a nearby college. Marcia was in nursing school at the time, working as a waitress on the weekends. Robin was hustling to get jobs in film while working at the coffee shop. They rarely saw each other, but the roommate situation worked well and they became fast friends.

"Robin, do you remember that day the faucet handle came off the kitchen sink and you ran to get the super? He showed up stoned with his sweat pants on backwards and a woman's blouse on? It was a weird place, but never once did I feel unsafe there."

"That was the moment I knew I wasn't in Kansas anymore," Robin chuckled. "It was bizarre. I think I had been in town about two weeks. I've seen college kids get stoned at parties before, but this was a whole new world. This guy looked like he hadn't seen daylight in decades. Nice enough, just odd. It takes all kinds, I guess."

Robin's apartment now was a stylish loft. The sleek, black

leather furniture with tubular frames, the large colorful artwork on brick walls, and shelves filled with books surprised Brooke. She thought of Robin more as a second-hand futon covered with a worn, colorful Mexican serape, a rescued rattan chair and a small television atop a painted bookcase kind of gal.

"Don't be so impressed. I had a couple friends leaving town. They didn't want to move their stuff, and they hooked me up with the landlord so I got first dibs on the place. They were happy their things went to someone they knew. Everything but the books. Most of those are mine. When I have downtime, that's what I do. You'll notice there's no television."

The loft style with the small balcony was perfect for entertaining the twenty guests who stopped in throughout the evening.

At the end of the evening, while Robin and Brooke cleaned up, Robin's friends Corrette and Stanley hung out and chatted. The three of them talked about excursions they took into Canada to raft and enjoy the outdoors. Corrette and Stanley were the first couple Robin befriended when she moved to the city.

"They pulled me out of my darkness more than once."

"Yeah, and to think it all started with one spilled cup of coffee." Corrette recounted the morning she stopped into the coffee shop where Robin worked. "It was crazy busy for a Sunday morning. Stan and I were grabbing a quick cup between our walk and church. Robin was new to town and I hate to say this honey, but you looked like death warmed over. You probably hadn't eaten in a couple of days and you clearly hadn't had a good night's sleep for a while."

"All true." Robin couldn't deny those early days left her scared, hungry and tired.

"Well, everything came to a head when she handed me my latte and it slipped out of her hand and through mine. I don't think we could repeat that move if we wanted to. Anyway, Robin looked at me with her chin quivering. 'I'm so sorry, let me make you a new one right away. I hope you didn't get any on you. Please, please, tell me I didn't burn you.' Tears streamed down her face."

"Right then, I knew we found another of our people." Stan took up the story. "I looked over at the owner, another friend of ours, and told him we were taking his new hire to church with us. He never batted an eye."

"That Hal was a wonderful boss. You work hard for him and the sky's the limit." Robin still stopped in to see him occasionally.

"I had a little warm coffee on my skirt but nobody was the wiser. By the time we got out of church it was dry and I smelled like freshly brewed coffee."

"That's not the end. You took me out to eat, let me crash in your guest room until I found a place to live, and have never stopped reminding me of that good cry over spilled milk I had. Really, you have been a Godsend to me."

Brooke loved a story with a happy ending. "Awe, Robin, you are so blessed."

"So now, Brooke, we need to know a little more about you. We already know that you're good folk just because you're kin, but *who* are you really?" From earlier conversation, Brooke knew that Stan was an adjunct English professor in the city and Corrette was a freelance illustrator for children's books.

"I have just left a management position in a boutique marketing firm in Miami. I led a team that most recently catered to restaurants. Previously I was the point person for a large hotel chain."

"Did you enjoy it?"

"I appreciated the opportunity they gave me to get managerial experience early in my career and the clients were great. The firm was built with a lot of integrity and was an excellent place to work, but I have developed a restlessness. I found myself a little sideways with the firm founder and decided it was time for me to move on. It was the best thing that could have happened. Now I see an immense opportunity to go out into the world and spread my wings!"

"So, that's cool and all, but *who* are you? You just told us about your work. Now tell us about you." Stanley had used this exercise with students who were stuck. It really helped him get to know them, but more importantly helped the students get to know themselves.

"Tough crowd, eh?" Robin winked.

Brooked grabbed her glass of wine and joined the couple at the dining table. "I am a twenty-something woman with a firm foundation in family values, integrity, an adventurous spirit, a small dose of anxiety and perfectionism, self-conscious about my round hips, freckled shoulders, bunions and twenty-minute mile."

"Well done. Now we are getting somewhere. What makes your heart sing?"

"I love to commune and create."

"Unpack that for me, will you?"

"Sure. This…" Brooke wagged her finger in a circle, indicating the four of them. "I love connecting one-on-one with people, getting to know them and listening to their stories. I also love to make music, bake cookies, write, entertain and laugh. What tops the list for me is the joy I feel when giving to or serving others. That's my sweet spot."

"Nice! So, how are you getting more of that into your life?"

"I think tonight was a grand start. I got to meet some brilliant people, make some fun food, and if there had been a karaoke machine I would have made some music. Robin, we need to get a karaoke machine."

"Noted." Robin was exhausted from the long day of shopping, cleaning and entertaining, but happy. "She has a fantastic voice. I can hum a melody, but she can stop the show with her pipes."

"Thanks, sis."

"Stan, honey, I think we should go and let these two beauties get their rest. Not everybody is a night owl like we are."

"I'm just getting started. Say, are you two interested in going ice-skating tomorrow? There's a rink about halfway between here and our house and a cozy little restaurant nearby with the best soups."

Brooke looked at Robin, her eyes begging her big sister to say yes. They skated a lot in their youth, but neither of them had skated much as adults.

"I will be a wreck on ice, it's been so long since I've been on skates." Robin's protest was weak.

"That's a yes. We'll be there. What time and where?"

Brooke's new enthusiasm for life was impressive and Robin didn't want to quash it. "OK. I'm not raining on anyone's parade. I'll be there, but probably not with bells on."

18

VIETNAM 2003

If you ever get the chance to travel through Vietnam, take it! This place is so beautiful and peaceful. I expected it to be a place where the people hate Americans, the land pockmarked with giant bomb divots, and the roads made of mud. None of this is true. The people here are exhausted from centuries of war and want only peace. They are kind and welcoming. The countryside is lush, and the cities are bustling. Today I floated the Ha Long Bay. The ethereal fog enveloping the island peaks rolled through my soul and deposited ancient drops of joy for me to carry forward. Watch for the jungle-wedding story next. This will certainly be nuptials like no other. Love and peace to each of you. I love your responses, and unless it's super private, respond to all so we can share your reactions with everyone.

Brooke sent photos and narrative to an email group she created back in January while still in New York. Friends and family appreciated her beautiful descriptions and photos. She used it to stay in touch, to explore writing. The emails became her writing prompts; a place to practice imagery and storytelling that she later turned into articles about each place she visited.

"I will not reply all. I just want to say, once again, thank you for sharing your stories. You are immensely talented, my dear friend. Love, Bridger."

Brooke loved it when she got a note from Bridger. She hadn't seen him since their chance meeting last October, nine months prior, but they kept in touch through email, texts and the occasional call. He recently learned that he would remain stationed in Germany for at least two more years. He was thrilled. *Hopefully your travels will bring you back to this part of the world and we can pick up where we left off.*

I would like that. Brooke had some 'practice dates', as she and Robin called them. They weren't really dates; she just went out for coffee or dinner with a couple of men she met in New York. When traveling, she met a lot of nice people and enjoyed great conversations, but there was nobody she formed a relationship with. She was happy just finding herself and enjoying a newfound confidence.

Besides near daily emails, she called her parents every other week. That was their request when she first started traveling alone. "It's so freeing to be in clothes that I choose to wear instead of those I have to wear for an office," she said on one of the calls.

"That's wonderful, honey. I'm glad you have this opportunity to get out there, explore the world, and be comfortable while doing it." Her mother didn't quite understand. She wore whatever she wanted on the ranch and dressed up, by choice, when she went to town. She never had to conform to a quasi-uniform. That's what business casual and business dress had become to Brooke - a uniform that looked similar to the uniforms worn by coworkers.

"Take today, for example," Brooke continued. "I'm wearing a bright orange top and loose purple harem pants and sandals. Can you imagine if I showed up at the office this way? And the humidity here is really making my hair curl."

"Oh, send me a picture! You know I love it when you don't straighten your hair. My friends in town love it when I bring them recent pictures or read your emails to them. Mrs. Kelly said to be sure to tell you hello. She's very proud of you, you know. She tracks down your articles and saves them."

"That's so sweet of her. She was my favorite teacher ever, but then she taught creative writing, my favorite subject. How's Dad doing?"

"He's good. He's right here and I'll pass the phone to him in a minute, but I just wanted to mention that I heard from Mrs. Goins. She said Bridger is staying in Germany a while longer. Do you have any assignments there?"

"Yes, he told me. I don't have any assignments, but I was thinking of calling that castle we visited and pitch my wedding idea to them. Maybe I can get a little marketing gig on the side with them. I would have done it before, but I've just been so busy and the work is flowing in right now."

"That's a brilliant idea. Well, here's your father."

Linda passed the phone to Frank. He and Brooke caught up on the happenings at the dairy farm. It comforted her to know that things were going well for her parents, at least from what they shared. "Lana and Pablo will come for a long weekend next month. That will be their first visit. We are looking forward to it. You know your mom. She's already filling the freezer with her excellent food."

"The reality is, you will probably go to town to eat out and show off the beautiful couple more than you will eat at home."

"Well, there's that, too." Frank knew Linda wanted her friends to meet Pablo and see how well Lana was doing for herself.

"When will Julie and the girls come visit?"

"Actually, the entire family will be here the first week in August, just before they go back to school. Keith got some time off then, too. I can't wait to have those little girls out here. I promised them a chance to ride the horses and feed the cows. Your mother will have Julie in the kitchen helping with the canning and Keith will take one of those old bamboo poles your grandpa made and toss it in the creek. He catches nothing, but boy does he like to fish."

"Good for him. I'm sure that solitude is a welcome reprieve for him. I'm sorry I will miss the canning this year, but my life is going so well right now that I couldn't ask for anything more."

"Well I'm so dang proud of you, honey, and wish you only the best."

"That's why you're my favorite pops. Well, I'm going now. There's a peanut soup calling my name and a late night massage I'm looking forward to."

"You stay safe, honey. Say, when do you think we'll see you again? Do you think you'll be home for Christmas?"

"I'm not really sure, Dad. There are so many interesting places to celebrate Christmas. It's just too soon for me to know. I will keep you posted though. Maybe you would like to join me."

"Well, I do kinda have that travel bug. In fact, I would like to get back to Germany and spend a little more time there. We had to rush through some beautiful places."

"We did, didn't we? I'll keep it in mind and let you know as we get closer."

Brooke was no longer in a position to pay for their trip. She was on a tight budget. Her work was steady, but she had not yet earned the right to charge big bucks for her work. Enjoyment of life was her biggest reward. "I'm really going now, Dad. Watch for my email tomorrow. I'll tell you all about the river trip into the jungle where the wedding will be in two days."

"Love you, honey. Have fun!"

"Love you and Mom too. Stay well."

Floating down the river, just an hour's bus ride from Ha Long, the boatmen transported us deep into the jungle. Much to my surprise, the boat landed at a dock at the base of a tall rock with one hundred steps to the top. Porters carried our luggage, running up and down the stairs with the ease of a skipping rock gliding over the water's surface. My new friends, the Rogers, are coming to the wedding from Los Angeles. The bride is their niece. They love to travel and inspired the bride's travel bug by gifting her with a trip when she graduated from high school. She actually met her soon-to-be husband on a trip she took in her early 20s. She was hiking in Peru and he was on the same trip. When she gradu-

ated from college, she joined him in Seattle and they have been living happily ever after.

I got this gig through a magazine featuring destination weddings. The resort comped the bride part of her stay, and did the same for me. In exchange they agreed to have me write the article and take some photos. It's a small wedding party, but a fun group! This is part of life's grand adventure for them.

The jungle and river are filled with exotic wildlife. Primates play on the rocks across the river, frogs and water monitors dot the shores and I hear tell of enormous snakes, but have not seen them yet. Flowering native plants bring color to the jungle. Vibrant orchids provide natural pops of color against the green. More to come post-nuptials . . .

19

—————

NEW YORK ~ 2003

*T*he editor for the magazine featuring destination weddings was thrilled with Brooke's work and offered her more engagements. She traveled from Vietnam to Cambodia, Thailand, and India in rapid succession. Three of those trips included wedding coverage for articles.

By late August Brooke looked forward to spending two weeks in New York with Robin.

Robin picked Brooke up at the airport, carrying the same backpack she had when she left months before. A small collection of boxes had arrived at Robin's apartment in the interim. "You look fantastic little sis!"

"I'm the happiest tired I've ever been. You look great yourself!"

"Why thank you. I'm feeling good. It's been pretty quiet since you left, what with no wild parties or anything, but I'm staying busy." Robin smiled to herself as she put the car in drive.

"Please tell me it's not all work."

"Hey, I'm not sure you're in a position to preach about working all the time. You've been gone how many months now?"

"If you think I'm working that whole time, you've got another think coming! I mean, I'm gathering impressions, information, photos and stuff all the time, but I'm not writing all the time or working the business side all the time. I've had lots of free time to explore and just live. It's been so refreshing and I feel the hard shell around my heart softening. I'm really loving this life."

"Now that's a story I would like to read! Are you working on something longer than a magazine article to share your story?"

"I am, but I've got a long way to go to flesh it out. It's a travel memoir, of sorts, but I'm weaving in the *before* me and the *after* me. There's still more soul searching to be done."

"I've been doing some of that myself."

"What's that?"

"Soul searching. I've been living a solitary existence for a long time, chasing my professional life."

"Oh, but you have put together a fabulous group of friends and you love your job."

"All of that is true, but I deserve to let love in my life, just like you. I told you it would be good to have you around, even if you're not right there every minute."

"So what are you saying?"

"I decided to let my hair down. Corrette and Stan have begged me for a while to meet a friend of theirs. I put them off and put them off, but after you left I decided why not?"

"Are you serious? Good for you. So, has this date happened? Tell me more."

"I think we're up to date sixteen or seventeen now."

"You go, girl! That's awesome."

Robin pulled into the apartment parking lot. "Let's finish this story upstairs. I made us some lunch."

"Who are you? What have you done with my sister?"

"I know, right? I feel like I've climbed out of this cave. It took a little time to get used to the light, but now that I see it I can't stop staring at it."

Brooke deposited her backpack on the bed and freshened up while Robin plated grilled tuna Nicoise salad and poured two glasses of sparkling water. She was excited to pull out the home-made raspberry cheesecake for dessert. She had become a regular Suzy Homemaker.

Fresh out of the shower with a change of clothes, Brooke sat down at the table. She was awed to see her sister's kitchen handiwork. "This is lovely, Robin. You really have turned a new leaf, haven't you?"

"I've been playing in the kitchen, yes. You know, it can really be a great decompresser from a stressful day."

"You digress. Let's talk about your new dating life."

"Would you like some fresh ground pepper? Here's some extra salad dressing if you want it. Do you see those cute little capers? I mean, I had the hardest time finding them in the store. I had to get help and the first young man had no more clue than I where to find them."

"Robin! Spill the beans."

"Justin. Justin Malley. He's the date, and he's been the date for two months now."

"Two months and you didn't say anything?"

"Yeah, isn't this fun? I wanted to tell you, but not in the flat electronic, no inflection or personality world. I wanted this. I wanted to see you react and for you to see my glow. I mean, right, there is a glow? People all around me say it."

"This fella has you tied in knots, hasn't he? He must be something special."

"Oh, yes, he's special. He's so special that he's cooking us dinner tonight. I really hope you didn't have other plans."

"Me? Plans? Ha! I need about three days to catch up on sleep and then I will start planning. Dinner sounds fabulous. But you still haven't told me anything."

"Taller than me, five years older, the kindest eyes you've ever seen, honest, authentic, wise, accomplished, athletic, spiritual, well-read, loves all types of music and old films, writes poetry, dances in his living room..."

"I think I'm starting to get the picture. Where is he, this cardboard cutout of the perfect man? I bet he's posing in his speedo on a beach somewhere, right?"

"You're funny. Justin is like nobody I've ever met before, except maybe Stan. They are a lot alike except Justin is younger. He is a music history professor at the same college and one of the youngest faculty members. I guess he's something of a prodigy in his field. He is new at this dating thing too. Like me, he was married to his work. He published a textbook last year and previously published two books of poems. He comes from a big family, most of whom are still living in Utah. He loves being outdoors and has taken me on some amazing hikes. I surprised myself. I could almost keep up with him when he's hiking at his slowest speed."

"Wow, this is like a whole new side of you I've never seen! Outdoors? Hiking? Cooking? Dancing?"

"Whoa. I said *he* dances. I still don't do that."

"I bet he's an excellent teacher, though. You'll learn."

They finished their salads and kept chatting as Robin cleared the table.

"No, you just sit. I have a little surprise dessert for us."

"Dessert? Robin, you're too much! It's like you've taken some sort of potion and unlocked all these magic rooms you've had closed off."

"It feels a little like that. This is only the second time I've made this, but I hope you like it." She presented Brooke with a perfect slice of baked cheesecake with brilliant fresh raspberries and white chocolate drizzle.

"Stunning! Absolutely stunning! I'm going to get you an apron for Christmas to finish this fresh look of yours."

"Speaking of Christmas, do you know what you will be doing?"

"I don't, and that's part of the planning I need to do over the next few days. I've been talking with the manager of this castle we visited in Germany about starting a destination wedding business. They are interested in my marketing services and have the opportunity to host a wedding for a prominent local family during Christmas Market sometime. That's when many of their family comes to town to sell handcrafts so they want to hold it then." Brooke savored a bite of the cheesecake. "This is fantastic! So, you bought a spring-form pan and everything?"

"I did. I found this great kitchen store and the gals there were so helpful. One of them gave me this recipe - it's their family's go-to. I learned about zesters and cocktail stirrers and fresh herb storage. You'll be surprised when you start poking around the kitchen. I have a few fun new things. Anyway, back to the castle."

"Where was I? Oh yeah, when I first started talking to them about destination weddings at the castle, it was spring and the ideas just flowed, but they weren't ready yet. They said they were too busy and pushed off planning until fall. Then this opportunity came up and now they want my services. I can do most of it from afar, but I will need to be there for the days leading up to the wedding and the actual event. I'm looking forward to it, I really am. But it means I probably won't be with Mom and Dad for Christmas again, unless they want to go with me."

"Does this mean you could see Bridger again? Wouldn't that be the icing on the cake?"

"I haven't said anything to him yet in case I can't come to a contract agreement with the castle. I am a little intimidated about seeing him again. I mean, I think I've changed and maybe this new me, with my hair down and my dungarees on, won't be what he's attracted to. Remember, when we first met I was wearing my business casual uniform. He thought I dressed smartly."

"Well, I'm sure your attire is not first and foremost to him. Your personality, your kind heart, and your beautiful voice, among other things, are what attract him. I understand not telling him yet. Why get his hopes up?"

"To be honest, I think I'm going to surprise him. Recreate our initial meeting but in Munich, this time. He loves Christmas Market and frequents certain places there. I think I can make it happen."

"You've spent a lot of time thinking about this, haven't you? You give off this air that you're only a little interested, but you really are crazy about this guy, aren't you?"

"If I believed in love at first sight, he would be it. Now that we have had months of getting to know each other without the distraction of physical attraction, I'm even more wowed by him."

"I've always thought he sounded like a wonderful guy and I know Mom and Dad are impressed with both he and his mother. Mom can be pretty picky."

"And Dad very protective."

"True. I think the only person who needs convincing is you and it sounds like that's happened."

"Well, there's the whole where would I live problem."

"How is that a problem? Your work takes you places, and you can always land here if you need to be in the States. Would it be so difficult to be headquartered in Munich?"

"No. In fact, it may bring additional opportunities. I don't want to rush into that, though. I haven't had that conversation with Bridger. I've been really noncommittal with him and that may be unfair. I'm not sure."

"You might be too hard on yourself. How could you be any more invested without actually having those critical face-to-face conversations?"

"You're right. No heart emoticon is strong enough to convey that message. And the more I think about things, I don't think I want to invite Mom and Dad to Germany if I get this gig. They will tell Mrs. Goins and then Bridger will know and I can't surprise him."

"Oh, you're right. Better to have that experience all to yourself. There will be another time, I'm sure."

"Well Robin, this is great! I love your glow. It's there. I see it. Tell me it's not just the guy, but that you've done some soul searching yourself.

"Of course I have. I've been involved in some very powerful indie films looking at life purpose, supernatural experiences in people of religion, and a bunch of other stuff. It really got me thinking, and talking to people, about faith, love, human relations, and mostly, perspective."

That sounds amazing. Let's talk some more, but first, let me help you with the dishes and then I've got some business to do before I take a nap. What time are we leaving for dinner? Will it just be the three of us?"

"Let me do the dishes. That's my therapy. It's about forty minutes to Justin's place, so let's plan to leave at about five."

Brooke gave her sister a hug. "Thank you. I'll be ready. Let me know if you need me before then."

SHE HEADED to her room to unpack, start laundry, and review her assignment list. She checked her email first: still nothing from the castle. She checked her phone for messages. *Hope you made it to Robin's safely. Beautiful day here. I went hiking after work with some friends. Be well, dear one.*

Arrived safe and sound. Have been fed and entertained. A little work, a nap, and off to meet Robin's new 'friend'. Sounds like you had a good day. Video chat tomorrow?

Bridger's response came almost immediately. *Absolutely!*

Brooke called her parents to let them know she was safe and sound. She introduced the idea of not being around for Christmas, since her dad asked, but made no commitment as to where she would be. "I know you asked about Christmas, Dad. I have a few irons in the fire right now that may take me out of the country, but I won't know until later what that will be. I think the safest thing to do would be to count me out of your festivities and maybe we could celebrate early or after the New Year."

"We will celebrate Christmas, as usual, but will definitely do something special with you whenever you're available. We're glad you made it home safely. Keep us posted on your next trip, please."

"I sure will."

Frank reported that all was well on the farm, but he sounded exhausted. Brooke asked her mom, who simply said that he was working late hours in the fields and had some repairs that pushed the milking schedule off, but there was nothing to be concerned about.

Brooke finished the call and went to find Robin. "Have you talked to Mom and Dad lately?"

"It's been a couple of weeks, why?"

"Dad just sounds so exhausted."

"What does Mom have to say?"

"She says he's just been working hard and long hours. Sometimes I don't trust them to be transparent, you know? Do you think we need to check on them?"

"I don't think you need to go. Julie's family will be there soon enough. Lana and Pablo visited not too long ago, and I didn't get a distress call from them, you know?"

"Got it. I am prone to worrying too much."

"I'll chat with them tomorrow. That's when I would normally call them."

"Thank you. That's why you're the best sister. You're calm and well reasoned… well… maybe. We'll see after I meet Justin tonight." Brooke chuckled and retreated to her room to rest.

20

On Saturday evening, December 20, Brooke stood leaning against the old stone wall of an eatery facing the Glockenspiel, watching the Christmas Market swell with shoppers. Merriment flowed through Marienplatz like water through a swollen river back home. Christmastime brought out the best in people, or at least that's how Brooke chose to see it. She saw handshakes, hugs and smiles all around. Children pointed to brightly colored toys. Mothers and fathers shopped for ornaments that would appear on their magical Christmas trees at home on Christmas Eve.

The large tree in front of Town Hall stood aglow, wrapped in thousands of tiny Christmas lights. Over one hundred wooden stalls filled St. Mary's Square. The snow blanketing the roofs reflected the lights from the tree, giving the scene a festive and romantic glow. A small group of carolers, in traditional dress, performed for passersby. Large lighted stars stood atop the lampposts carrying the light into the night sky.

Brooke had landed in Munich three days earlier and drove to Heidelberg Castle to tour the wedding venue. The contract was finalized. This was her one shot with them to develop a marketing campaign for the venue and potentially open several doors in the destination wedding industry. She met with the bride and groom, the castle manager, the caterer and wedding planner over those three days. Today she had presented a series of color and font schemes to the Castle manager and a local art director. The meeting was a monumental success, and she was now free for the next two days. The wedding would be on December 23; she needed to be back at the castle then, ready to mingle, interview, gather information, and take photos.

Bridger didn't know she was in town. He thought she was spending time with family for the holidays and that's where he'd sent her gift. She felt horrible for not being honest, but wanted to surprise him. She hoped her plan wouldn't backfire and leave her surprised instead! With effort, she put aside the insecurities and went with the feeling, deep in her gut, that he would be as happy to see her as she would him.

Bridger told her earlier in the week that he was joining a colleague in the Square on December 20. The colleague had family visiting from back home and knew that Bridger was the best local tour guide. He gladly agreed to join them, always happy to visit the Christmas Market. He had favorite Christmas shops, knew some vendors and where to get the best mulled wine, gingerbread and special wares. It would not really be a long shot to expect to see him at the evening display of the Glockenspiel at nine.

Shoppers filled the square, carrying bags and sipping mulled wine or warm cocoa to ease the coolness of the evening. As show time approached, most faced the Town Hall and looked up, waiting for the night watchman and child's angel to appear.

Not too far away, Brooke heard a familiar voice above the dull roar of the crowd. "This vignette is called bedtime for the Bavarian child. When the night watchman blows his horn three times, curfew has fallen. The angel floats out and blesses the city."

Brooke moved along the building toward the voice, which came from a small group standing just outside the larger crowd. She stood back, waiting for the performance to end and the crowd to thin. As it did, Brooke pulled her hat down over her forehead, walked closer to the group, stood several feet away from Bridger, and opened the travel guide clutched tightly in her gloved hand.

She studied the page, looked up to the buildings around her and mimicked her motions in Amsterdam when she was genuinely lost and looking for street signs. She slowly crept closer to Bridger's group. She could hear the small group around him thank him for his guidance during the evening. The group was making plans to meet the following day and explore some of the churches in the area.

As Bridger bid the American guests a good night, he glanced her way. In the glowing lights of the square, he noticed the silhouette of a woman studying a map. He had spent the evening touring guests around and, as was his nature, thought maybe he could be of assistance.

"Excuse me ma'am. It looks like you're looking for something. Can I help?"

"Mmm-hmm. I'm looking for Temple Bar…" She paused to let the grin grow across his face before she looked up and turned toward him.

"I believe, ma'am, you are in the wrong country."

Brooke stood before him in the glow of the Christmas lights, more beautiful than he remembered, if that was possible. "This! This moment is magic! Look at you, bathed in Christmas glow! Beautiful… can I kiss you?"

"If you don't, I'm going to feel really silly. I didn't come all this…" Before she could finish Bridger wrapped her in his embrace, and she enjoyed the most romantic moment one could ever imagine. He was everything she remembered, and so much more.

Bridger slowly pulled back and looked into Brooke's eyes. "Now, may I ask what brings you to town, beautiful?"

"Yes, but I'm not exactly sure how to answer. I came for a wedding, but the real attraction was to see you. Could we find a place around here to warm up and talk?"

Sipping hot tea and sharing a pretzel in a late night restaurant, Brooke explained her pursuit of Heidelberg Castle's wedding marketing business and the upcoming-featured wedding. "I don't suppose you could escort me to the wedding, could you? It's not fair of me to spring…"

"I would love to be your escort! I have several days off for the holidays and my only obligation is to meet my colleague and his guests tomorrow. You're welcome to come along and tour the churches if you'll still be in town." He paused to take in the surprise of her. "There's something different about you. Wonderfully different. The sparkle in your eye is dancing more boldly."

"Well said! I feel lighter, more engaged in life. Honestly, I have a better sense of confidence and the things I used to fear now seem frivolous."

"All of that looks great on you. It is just so good to see you! I thought you were with family for Christmas."

"Bridger, I'm sorry about that. I didn't mean to deceive, really I didn't. I just had it in my head that I wanted to surprise you."

"Well, you sure did that! Best surprise of my life!" Bridger lifted Brooke's hand in his and kissed it. "The very best."

EPILOGUE
MUNICH ~ 2004

*R*obin wore a porcelain-colored, sleeveless lace gown with a fitted bodice, a frothy tulle skirt, and sheer back with pearl buttons. She slipped her hand into Brooke's. "You've done it, sis. This is all magic, and to be walking down the aisle with my best friend is the icing on the cake. I can't believe this is me here. I still remember those pictures you sent from that first wedding you helped with here. You made everything look like a fairytale, just like today. And me, the least sentimental person in the world, was so taken with the elegance of it all."

"You can't deny that you have changed… a lot… over the past year. Before you met Justin you wouldn't have dreamt of a tulle skirt let alone a wedding in a castle. He had really awakened something in you."

"That's for sure. I mean, when I first met him, I liked him but thought he was a bit geekish. You know, like me. And he is. We are. But the romantic in him is just so warm and inspiring. I mean, at our age, who would have thought he would ask Mom and Dad for my hand? It's charmingly old-fashioned. And, what about you and Bridger! I have never seen a happier bride, Brooke, and you've been beaming since you first met him. I wasn't the least bit surprised when you decided to move to Munich."

"Really? I wasn't at all sure until I had been here for a while. I think my hesitation had more to do with Mom and Dad than with Bridger and I."

Brooke ran a hand across the smooth silky dress before taking her bouquet from their shared Matron of Honor, Lana. She toyed with the crystal beads on the waistband. Her gown was a gift from one of the vendors she worked with. It was far more elaborate and expensive than she would have ever chosen, but she loved it and knew the wedding photos would be magazine-worthy. The cashmere-colored dress boasted a tastefully plunged bodice with a hint of corsetry providing for a modest cleavage view. Appliquéd vines fell from the shoulders to the elbows, carrying over from the bodice. Jeweled buttons dotting the illusion back, giving way to sparkling sequin lace appliqués on the skirt. Typically camera-shy, Brooke was so excited about marrying Bridger that she couldn't help but glow and smile the entire day.

The duo chose to marry in the late summer knowing their mother would love to be back in the country when many of the flowers were in bloom. Brooke had taken the laboring oar to make arrangements with the castle, which was perfectly fine with her. She had formed great relationships with the staff, who had become her greatest allies in the industry. She had a lucrative year with her freelance marketing and writing services. Bridger was incredibly supportive and walked every step of the wedding planning with her to get to this epic day of celebration.

Brooke looked down the aisle. She smiled at their mother and father who were basking in the fanfare. She looked across the aisle to Bridger's family. Both families had spent the past week touring the country and enjoying getting to know one another.

Finally, she looked toward the sanctuary. Her breath caught in her throat as she saw the two men standing at the ready to receive them, Justin looked handsome in his formal black tux with a porcelain vest. Bridger was in his dress blues, standing tall and strong. Her prince charming!

"Oh my! Look at those handsome men waiting for us at the

front of the chapel on the other end of this ancient stone walkway! They really are the best part of this whole affair."

The sisters shared a smile and a quick hug as the chamber orchestra struck the first notes of Mendelssohn's Wedding March.

"I love you."

"I love you too, sis."

They nodded to their father, looking dapper in his tuxedo, to escort them down the aisle. Their mother was the first to stand as the processional started. Her joyful smile beamed as her beautiful daughter, including Lana, the matron of honor for both sisters, gracefully glided down the aisle.

ROBIN AND JUSTIN were first to exchange vows. They elected to use traditional vows, promising to love, honor and cherish one another. Theirs was a beautiful exchange and fitting for them. Brooke and Bridger loved telling the story of how they met and wanted to bring that story into their wedding vows. They spent weeks sharing ideas, reading old email and text message exchanges and writing their story. Then they condensed it into vows.

"Here today, in the presence of our loved ones in this beautiful castle where surely God is present, I make these promises to you, Brooke, my love. I promise to come to your rescue whenever you are lost, to smile when you sing, to grow with you in ways that will strengthen our marriage and bring us closer to God." Bridger spoke in earnest while holding Brooke's hand in his. "I promise to love your family, as my own, and to forever support you in your heartfelt endeavors."

Brooke trembled slightly as she started her vows. She was touched by Bridger, and even more so by the gentle way he held her hands and looked into her eyes. "Bridger, my love, with you I am at home, whether traveling the world or in your physical presence at home in Munich. I am blessed to have found you, with your brilliance, warmth, generosity, and love for life. I promise to always be available for adventure, to share my heart openly, to build a life in Christ with you. I promise to take the road less traveled, if you want, and to find new ways to love you and show you that love every day.

ACKNOWLEDGMENTS

Sending gratitude to Denise, for sharing your chance encounter. Thank you to my editor and coach, Linda Zeppa of Intuitive Writing. Your inspiration, guidance, and intuition never fail me. To Angela of Angela Pruden Proofreading, I appreciate you and your great attention to detail. To Brenda of Blue Valley Author Services, thank you for you perfect cover design.

ABOUT THE AUTHOR

Kim Smart is a storyteller, nurse, attorney, and student of life. *Christmas Market Reunion* is her sixth published novel. Kim's fiction works incorporate personalities, experiences, and narratives from her life and the lives of friends and family. Kim has been a lifelong writer and today weaves in stories of the characters she meets at home and across the globe. Kim was raised in South Dakota and *grew up* in Alaska where her next series, *The Lynx Creek Chronicles*, is set.

You can learn more at www.kimsmartauthor.com or through the social media links below.

ALSO BY KIM SMART

Tangled Ribbons

War and the Holocaust tear three young girls from their youthful innocence.

Catapulted into their new lives, they become extraordinary women of resilience, grit and grace.

An unrelenting pursuit of forgiveness and peace for humanity follows.

The essences of individual humans are substantially more alike than they are different. Gertie Hall lives this truth as she rises from the young child of a Hitler henchman to a world-renown advocate for human rights. Through scientific endeavors, humanitarian efforts and a tireless fight to right the wrongs of her father, she explores her feminine self, intellect, ingenuity, and grit.

A hole remains in her soul where war ripped two childhood friends away, and Gertie's own father was complicit in the disappearance of their families. Tangled Ribbons, scene by scene, captures the life of Gertie, intertwined with the stories of her friends, Sarah and Hannah, who flee fiery Berlin and establish new identities and new lives in faraway places.

Late in their lives, Gertie offers a heart-wrenching plea for amends and enfolds a new generation in their healing.

If you love to read about inner strength, the pursuit of justice, and the power of friendship, you'll love *Tangled Ribbons*.

Get Kim Smart's *Tangled Ribbons* now and experience the journey of healing.

Falling for Home

Jesse loves his hometown girl...

Kerry has dreams beyond Buffalo Ridge...

..can they both have it all?

Jesse loves the ranch life as much as he loves his hometown sweetheart.

As they drift apart, he finds himself following a winding path searching for life's meaning.

To find love, he must first find his voice.

Kerry's dreams are larger than Buffalo Ridge. To pursue her dreams, she leaves everything behind. Her pursuit to become a veterinarian consumes her. Opportunity for lasting love disappears. Will she find her way back?

Can two small-town friends find happily-ever-after?

You'll love the dance of life and tug of emotions as Jesse and Kerr test boundaries in this first novel of Kim Smart's Buffalo Ridge Ranch series.

Get this sweet, clean, contemporary romance now.

Two for Love

A handsome widower cowboy, a woman from the city with a son, and the wide open spaces of the colorful Badlands.

Steve Davies lives his life in the shadow of his late wife's dreams. To emerge from his grief, he must take a chance. Hoping to expand the dreams they had together, he starts a dude ranch. In the process, he hires a cook - a city girl who brings along her son.

Bella Giordano needed to find safety for her young son. On a whim, she moves them from Manhattan to the Badlands of South Dakota, hoping the small town life, away from mob threats and smog, will be good for them both.

Will grief dissolve and a new opportunity be enough to build a new family?

The second novel in Kim Smart's Buffalo Ridge Ranch series sets the table for new opportunities and the possibility of love. Will hurts heal and love grow?

Taking Chances

Chance Davies, champion bull rider, goes from being rock star of the rodeo to broken and lost after a final ride turns into a tragic accident. He is forced to return to Buffalo Ridge Ranch for recuperation after many years on the circuit. Through hard work and challenging himself, his body starts to heal. But will he allow his mind and spirit to heal and open up to new opportunities?

Sheltered from love, Pauline Whyte was always a misfit in the small town of Buffalo Ridge where everyone knew her family's business. She escaped the town gossip for a few years by moving away, only to have to return to care for her ailing father. Somehow, in this small town, love finds its way to her. Can she accept it?

To let love in, they must overcome loss and pain. Will her misfit ways fit into his new life for a happily-ever-after?

The third novel in Kim Smart's Buffalo Ridge Ranch series brings a story of overcoming the odds. Is that enough to find true love?

Dressing Up Stella

Stella Davies lived far away from Buffalo Ridge Ranch. Fearing repeat abandonment, she built the life of a cowboy nurturing her herd on the rugged edge of nature in Arizona. But to find happiness, she must face these fears. When she moves to the remote high desert, she is forced to face her fears.

Ranching was in Brandon Cage's blood, but a new career as a lawyer changed his focus. He buried himself in his new profession and totally ignored his heart's desires.

Do they have the gumption to clear the way to give love a chance? Will their love arrive in time to find a life happily-ever-after?

The fourth novel in Kim Smart's Buffalo Ridge Ranch series is about overcoming past hurts and prioritizing love.

www.ingramcontent.com/pod-product-compliance
Lightning Source LLC
Chambersburg PA
CBHW050540190726
48284CB00003B/1148